Other books by Sherrie DeMorrow:

The Knight and Daye series:

Knight and Daye
Cloud of Dreams
The Elder Rose
All The Land
The Little Bird
Beyond the Land
A Little Princess
Romancing the West
The Silver Millions
The Painted Chapel
A Hound's Desire
Space of Things

The Young Dr Huer series

A Beginners Realm
Flight Into Space

FLIGHT INTO SPACE

BY

SHERRIE DEMORROW

Published 2021 by

Lightning Source (UK) Ltd
Chapter House,
Pitfield,
Kiln Farm,
Milton Keynes
MK11 3LW,
UK

Dr Huer character and Buck Rogers in the 25th Century©, tm by the Dille Family Trust, All Rights Reserved

Buck Rogers in the 25th Century TV series© Universal Studios, All Rights Reserved

Any place names or characters from the TV series were used solely as reference, with no intention of infringement of intellectual property rights of the aforementioned.

All rights reserved. No part of this publication may be reproduced, stored in a retrieval system, or transmitted, in any from or by any means, electronic, mechanical, photocopying, recording or otherwise, without the prior permission of the publishers.

© Sherrie DeMorrow 2021

Cover Art Design by Sam Wall

*In Memory of Tim
With love*

PREFACE and AUTHOR'S NOTE

Please be advised this novel is a continuation of a backstory of the character of Dr Elias Huer of the *Buck Rogers in the 25th Century* series, old and new, but I am basing it on the television series that aired from 1979-81. However, the events in this story PREDATE the television series, and cover Dr Huer's younger years, up until the series itself. Then the story ends.

I did write to gain permission from Universal to use this character, but I got no answer. Hence, I am writing these new series of books in loving tribute to the man who portrayed Dr Huer in the television version, Tim O'Connor. Tim has made appearances in several of my books, re-imagining a character for him in the *Knight and Daye* series that I just completed. This story does draw from those books, to put a cohesive backstory to the Dr Huer character. I want to give the man more than just a 'desk job'. I want to see what his early years were like, for example: what he thought, how he lived. Was the 25th century all that it was cracked up to be, as it was shown on television? Why did Dr Huer seem so sad? I want to see the good doctor in action, like Buck Rogers from the previous shows. A lot of the time, the doctor was so dead-pan serious, it made me wonder. An actor of the older generation would display vast amounts of seriousness to a role that was expected to be serious. However, the portrayal was so good, it made the character dull and boring. I do not believe (and I refuse to believe) that he was really like that. There is much to explore, and to examine the nature of Dr Huer is an excellent example of fandom, indeed.

Some place names and characters given are based on the television series (like New Chicago, or Anarchia, Kane and Twiki); acknowledgements for this had been made previously. Other characters, mentioned or otherwise, are fictional and loosely based on people known of by the author, or from the previous *Knight and Daye* series. Any personalities referred to herein are used (again), in loving tribute.

If there is anything amiss, please write to the publisher, and it shall be corrected.

CHAPTER I

I returned home to an unwilling reunion. A unification of non-spirits together in one vast horde. Unwilling, because my father was no longer with
us. While I enjoyed my days with Cindihan, even planning to marry her, I
felt the loss of my father. It was hard to bear, a grizzly one at best. I was
dumbfounded with it, yet with a yearning to get on and be with Cindy.

I was fiddling around in the old bedroom. She was there, looking at the
bookcases, which fascinated her. Where she lived in Anarchia, you were
lucky to even see a book, much less read one! It was the old bedroom Silage and I once shared together, growing up. Now that he's on Dracos doing some hard core learning, I opened myself up to Cindy. I also showed
her the fuss that was made between a bunch of history books, and my
brother. The Saturn moon was no match for him. I would dislike imagin-
ing what trickery he'd ensure with all his knowledge of the past.

'She looked at one in particular with fascination; it was the Irish mythology
and history book, I remember Silage reading when he was a child. 'Can I
read this?

'Go right ahead,' I dismissed, 'You're very welcome to it. Maybe you will
understand my brother better than me.'

Cindy became unnerved and came close to me. 'Elias, I do not want to hurt
you. After all we'd been through with Eri-Cast, and Barkhor, there should
be nothing that could separate us.'

Nothing that could separate us? What did she mean by that??

'Elaborate, please,' I dared her.

'Well,' she began, with a pause that was anticipating a pregnancy that was long overdue. 'I can sense you feel hurt by this volume. From what I gather, your brother took interest in it and you did not. As you did not share his interest with him, it put you into a distant position from him. You went separate ways, so to speak, early on, and it shows in your upstart attitude. Maybe your personalities.'

'Maybe, but you had not met him yet, if at all,' I replied, partly to myself. 'You didn't know what he was like. But I did look through the volume once; you can have a look now, if you want.'

My anticipation knew no bounds, as I did not know how it would affect her. *Or would it?* She seemed too practical in mind, concentrating on the moment, not dealing with elaborate witchery spells or demonic conjurings or other nonsense of the like. I liked her for that; it was critical for scientific work to *be* like that. Otherwise, what would science be like, if not to fend for our future souls? Practicality was a must in the field. I tried to imagine space flight based on magic… *nah, it wouldn't wash!*

Cindy looked up at me, 'Will you read them with me?'

'And mess up my scientific mind with archaic crap? No, thank you,' I retorted.

She looked dismayed. The book shown much promise. My life with Cindy did too, but this was beginning to become a tension point. I really did not wish to get into this with her.

'It's you I want, Elias, not your brother,' she comforted me with a hug.

'Besides,' she continued, 'I think it would be better if we *did* study this on our own, or something, as it may prove useful, in case we have a run-in with him.'

'Like I'm going to Dracos? Hah,' I spat. 'I wouldn't set foot there in another five hundred years! And what makes you think I would have a run-in with him, eh? How?'

'Don't dismiss the concept so easily,' she warned. 'People always bump into one another, whether or not with intent. In Anarchia, I've seen it before.'

I got curious now. 'Seen what before?'

'People fighting it out. People knowing what the other one thinks or what makes them tick. People betraying one another, despite them knowing one another, like, *forever*!'

I got it. Cindy understood the baseness of human nature, but not all of it. It was filled with disgusting attributes like greed and lust, slightly embedded evil, too. It made me shrink to know that my little lovely innocent Cindy was much more than what she offered. It was even scarier to know that she knew those ugly sides of Mankind. The sides that were willing to activate the detonator, which caused the Big Blast in the instance. Unfortunately, all this negativity made me unhappy for the things she'd been through and gave her a willing hug to make it right.

'There is a shinier side to things, you know,' I mused, begging to galvanize her.

'Like what?'

'Oh,' I continued my parley into decorative thought, flowering myself into defending my home city. 'The way we are here in New Chicago is spotless, pristine, and glowing, even, and we've learned to work together as a team. We have keen academies, we have Computer Councils, we have...'

'... *and you have nothing*,' she ranted at me. 'You are no different from the people I left behind. Sure, you may *do* things differently around here, using computers to do your dirty work, but you are still no different. Human nature is human nature, and all I can say for it is that it sucks!'

Well, that caused a sensation in me that I did not expect.

I then tried to smile at her, after all that. 'You pick up on things, don't you?'

It threw her off, but she remounted quickly. 'You have to, in order to survive in Anarchia, to survive *anywhere*.'

I let the dear girl peruse the book as I whistled by the window. I stared out into the space that was before me; what did I see? Many buildings of shapes that would baffle an ancient mathematician, vehicles that whirred on rails or free-for-all in the air; fighter jets that hissed away into the outer stratospheres, and into the stars; street lights that were dimly glowing in the early evening sky, rivalling the Computer Councils' 'Christmas light' encasements. Everything was a-buzz and filled with life. It made old New York seem quiet during their evening rush hour. Maybe she was right in all things. *Maybe...*

'It says here that Muffyhuer and Cindihan were rulers of Cobhayr, before they were engulfed by the earth and its gods.

'The town was later renamed Oconnalow in their honour,' Cindy read out loud, then glanced at me. 'Are you the new Muffyhuer?'

I huffed back, 'How can I be, if Muffyhuer was taken by the gods and swallowed up by a cave or something?'

A disquieting pause overtook us. Then, I approached her romantically. 'Are you the new Cindihan?'

Her smile was enigmatic. 'This must be the Cindihan whom I was named for, by those in Anarchia,' she carried on reading. 'A magical potion stayed his age until his dying breaths, when he became ninety in an instant.'

'Goes to show you, it's a bunch of trollop-wash. Utter nonsense,' I waved my hand.

She continued on, 'A spell was used by making...'

I got impatient at the passages. 'Okay, okay.' I took the book off her and put it down, and held little Cindy. 'Let's forget these things for now; it could be dangerous. This is more than millennial-old stuff. We've come quite far since then.'

'Okay,' she sighed quietly. 'Can we play a game?'

'Wha--?' I stopped suddenly, when a small chime sounded, and Pemur entered the room.

He called out, 'Hello?'

'In here, Oppenmach,' I responded.

He went further past the doorway, and unto a lit seat, which he rested on. 'I'm sorry about your father,' he said, 'He was a good man, even better for New Chicago.'

'Yeah, I know, 'I sighed.

I felt the loss, as I felt earlier, but I didn't want it to take over my life.

I continued, 'There is a new wind afloat and we must meet it.'

Pemur suddenly perked up. 'Really? Who?'

'Cindihan,' I exclaimed.

He looked over at the dear lady, sitting there. She went back to looking at the history book again. She read to herself this time, and I questioned whether to let her keep at it.

'Hiya, Cindy,' Pemur called to her, 'What are you reading?'

She got up and showed him the volume. 'We're in this. I was named for the Cindihan in this book. Elias's ancestor changed the family name to Huer from Muffyhuer.'

'Wow,' he said, taking the book and looking through it, noticing the names we referred to. He then joked, 'Seems you both have muffled commonal-ity.'

Ha-ha. The two of them were captured by the text and read along together, learning about the pretty stuff that captured my twin brother's heart. It made me a bit sad to watch Pemur getting into all the story like Silage did. They looked at one another in a studious overtone and conversed, which I did not want to get involved with. So, I remained distant, as not to encapsulate my mind with nonsense that has no further meaning than that of a playtime story. I puttered around, cleaning the place off.

'Elias, you know you can stay here with Cindihan, if you want. Your experimentation can continue.'

I cried, 'But, I haven't begun to experiment yet!'

'You will, you will,' Pemur gave me a sly smile. He knew what he was thinking.

And so did I.

The possibility for me to take over Dad's work, maybe joining the Directorate, was not far from his thought. Pemur knew how important Dad was in rebuilding New Chicago, as well as others before him. He was thinking I would take over the business, so to speak, so as to continue the life-breeding in the scientific world, we all knew and loved.

'Very funny,' I pouted.

He raised a different topic, with a similar subject. 'What are your plans then?'

My thoughts banged in, and pointed at Cindy. 'As if you didn't know.'

Pemur got it, and laughed. 'I figured you'd want her. Anything else?'

'Yeah,' I said, 'Flying.'

'You can go flying for the Directorate anytime.'

Cindy looked up to see me and Pemur wrangling out about her. 'I didn't think I would be the subject of desire and provocation.'

'You are, my dear,' I went over to her and cooed, 'But you're not. Oppen-mach was just curious as to our intentions. Why you're here and such.'

'I'm here, because you brought me here,' she replied.

'That's right. I chose to get you out of your anarchic existence and into something much healthier.'

Pemur threw a fireball at us. 'Meantime, what about your father?'

I turned my head. 'What about him?'

'Well, there is something called a funeral, which is still required in this century,' he twiddled his thumbs in amusement.

'I can do that,' I uttered.

'You don't sound enthused,' Pemur added.

'No, I wish to marry Cindy,' I fought back.

'Alright. Don't get your circuits blown out. Leave it with me. I'll help you.'

He extended his hand out; I shook on it.

'Thank you,' I accepted the kind offer.

I decided to leave it. Let Pemur and company do the funeral arrangements. I dreaded to think what Silage would have to say about this, once informed. I was half-masted anyway, and wasn't in the mood for a funeral in the first place. Death was something to be relished by the individual going through it. Everyone else was obligated to remember the person, but not to go on and on about it. I had more dire needs awaiting me.

CHAPTER II

In addition to the funeral, Cindy and I planned our wedding. It didn't take much, and Cindy already made a new friend called Jensley Gale, who was not only happy to assist, but willing to be her bridesmaid. She wasn't too jealous, and her dark eyes told me so. Her dark hair shouldered upon her like a cape. She was also very beautiful; unfortunately, not my type. She had a lover called Vince Tigman, who she'd been seeing for some time anyway. Tigman wasn't much more than a security fellow in the Directorate. He loved tattoos and proudly displayed them when out-of-uniform. Jensley enjoyed the time when he shared his tattoos with her. It was as if they were on an island alone together.

I asked Pemur to include an invite to our wedding, as well as informing of Dad's death, to Silage. If he comes, fine; if he doesn't, well, it would show how much of a brother he was to me. It would be nice to see him there, fresh from a Draconian Academy, no doubt. I would rather he be here, so I could keep tabs on him to prevent any mischief-playing on his part. I was a bit afraid to think if he had learned anything from Draconian history, fused with his knowledge of the various cultures of ancient Earth. No telling what this fellow was capable of.

Even though I wasn't part of the Directorate yet, at this time, my wedding outfit reflected a uniform of some sort. Pemur and I went for a trip out to the tailors to measure up for the big day. Brighter than the Directorate dullness of navy blue, or black, my outfit shone beautifully in pale blue, with a white trim. I liked it a lot, because it matched my eye colour and thought Cindy would go nuts for this sort of thing.

'Remember Elias,' Pemur warned, 'Do not forget the funeral that requires your attendance.'

'I know, and I will,' I assured him, still strapped in my wedding kit, looking extremely pleased with myself.

Deep down, I wanted to defy Pemur. Not that I wanted to detract from Dad's memory, but it was difficult to plan for both. I hated Pemur for reminding me of such things, but I didn't despair. I bucked it all off and focused away from the angry distraction. I went back to thinking about Cindy; I truly wanted her, *oh my!* I liked reflecting upon her surname, mimicking the old call people did whenever her original family appeared to the ancient Irish. I did not know what dress she would pick out for the wedding, but it didn't matter to me. She'd look exquisite in anything. That is how much I thought of her.

She went out with Ms Gale to fix herself a fine garment. I was later told it would have a *fairy queen* approach to it. A full cream coloured gown, with a slightly low neckline and three-quarter sleeves. The surrounding fabric was a light chiffon, making the look ethereal. As much as I would have loved to have been there, I thought it best to let her be. I guess the look was subliminally affected by her namesake of long ago. Maybe Cindy really wanted to be *her*. I certainly hoped not. If she was *that* Cindihan in reality, then I'd hate to imagine what would happen to me!!

When it came time for the funeral, I needn't dress up for it as such. I had a plain boring Directorate black suit affair, that was kept for just-in-case moments like this one. It was buttoned up to the top, bordered by dark coloured embroidery. Old, scientific colleagues were present, to see the great man off. Cindy held me and supported me the whole way. At least she was there for me. I was later informed Silage couldn't make the funeral. Haha. What a surprise.

He had to remain on Dracos; he had exams to take. As I slopped my way through the funeral, I would have liked him here with me. Desire proved too much when it came to family time, but it was good of him to send his regards. There was a possibility I'd deal with him at my wedding. I wasn't sure about his intentions yet, but he seemed sincere enough. I still missed him, whatever the strategy he chose to take.

As the funeral came and went, my mind quickly focused solely on the wedding, whose time had already come. It wasn't like I knew all of New Chicago, but some people of prominence had to attend this. The old scientific community was crowding over the area, due to seeing me off into manhood. They were proud of me, and it showed in their support. Some of Dad's friends and other colleagues showed up too. Everyone wondered about how little Elias, Jr would get on.

The only real friend I had, aside from Cindy, was Antssarah. I thought about him and his brother, and mine. My heart turned heavy, thinking whether they were really coming or not. Silage did indicate he would try to take time to see us. I guessed in reality he really wanted to meet Cindy. And I couldn't blame him. Cindy was a fine girl. I was so proud to wed the catch I made in Anarchia.

I looked around at the guests, whom none I knew. This embarrassed me. Pemur did a great job at filling the church and all, but it would have been nice to fill it with those I *knew*. As a best man, Pemur stood by me.

The rings were tucked away in a pocket, ready for when required. I wondered who would bring Cindy down the isle for me. I looked at Pemur for an explanation. There was none. Then I saw Lt Clary Busdon, waiting in the back with Cindy. It was a surprise to see Busdon in position to fulfil a task he can readily do, and he was pleased to do it. I thought Busdon and Pemur should switch roles, because it would have made more sense, but there you go.

Nothing was as it seemed.

I nodded to Busdon, and he acknowledged the nod, as he walked with her down the aisle to me. He still remained his shining best, and looked very vintage in his all-in-one coloured suit. His face looked square and sharp, something like a model from a magazine; a poster boy in the flesh. *Wow.* He looked more of a bridegroom than I did!

The minister read out his passages, reshaped for our time, and asked us the following questions.

'Do you, Elias Huer, Jr, take this woman Cindihan O'Myde, to be your law-fully wedded wife?'

I nodded, 'I do.'

'Do you, Cindihan O'Myde, take this man, Elias Huer, Jr, to be your law-fully wedded husband?'

She exclaimed, with jubilation that was hard to miss. 'I do!'

'Then seal your bargain with a kiss. Congratulations and peace be with you both,' he concluded.

The minister then left us to go to the vestry. His words were pleasant and I figured he meant well for us. I knew what we did was nothing to sniff at, and soon enough, Cindy turned to me.

'We did it,' she joyfully screamed.

'I know, I know, little one,' I teased her, regarding her small stature. 'Be it ever so exciting.'

The people present applauded us, as did Pemur and Jensley.

Busdon came up to me and jokingly asked, 'May I have the first dance?'

'Sure,' I smiled at him. 'It's nice to see you helping us.'

'It was a pleasure, Elias,' Busdon flashed a smile at me.

We were ushered down the isle, to show off that we were now one. I was elated, I looked forward to a new life with Cindy.

Hopefully, the flying lessons would permeate soon afterwards. I just couldn't wait to get into orbit. Suddenly, I was tripped in the mind about a few people we spotted at the rear of the church. A small party stood there, dressed differently from everyone else. Upon closer inspection, my heart leaped a beat when I realised who they were: Silage and the Kane brothers.

CHAPTER III

As it turned out, the Kanes and Silage *did* come to the wedding. We were a lot older now, or at least *felt* it. Dracos took care of its own, and the school allowed Silage and the Kane brothers a short break to attend my wedding. It was bad enough Silage missed the funeral, but it was good of the school to make up for it.

They looked snazzy in flashy coloured, sequin suits, with Silage taking the lead. He did look different, with a one piece, dark coloured suit, cut in the middle to show himself off. *What can I say?* He was more daring than I remembered. I reckoned it was from all that book reading about the ancients that gave him the confidence in himself. It certainly brimmed to the fore. He looked a treat to all the ladies standing in our presence, and it make it seem that *he* was the belle of the hour.

The new siren of the stars approached me. 'Brother Elias, how are you? I am most pleased to see you found your manly way.' He then beamed at me, and had a good look at my new wife, Cindihan Huer. 'Your tastes are astonishing. Never would I have imagined a scientist-to-be experimenting with a ravishing beauty.'

He kissed Cindy's hand, as I stood by and watched seethingly, my teeth clenched, the mind curdled, as if... *Never mind, it was a wedding after all.* Silage did grow into a very handsome man, with a keen mind and wit. I didn't think he'd make eyes at *her*. She was just a child, with a grown up sense of being; old enough to call her own, but still thought of herself as youthful.

Cindy took a back seat in all this, taking it in, with her acute senses. I guessed being in Anarchia gave her insight that served her in many a situation. Reading people was one thing she was renowned for.

This situation, though, was to be a good testing ground for her. She now understood why I loved referring to him as Silage.

'You are extremely charming, sir,' she beamed back with his own precision. 'Your countenance does you good.'

'Your grace and beauty belong among the Draconian forests,' he cooed at her, 'You should see them at night. It is just like what I've read about. You may call me Silas.'

'Thank you,' she said.

Silage and I exchanged glances before Cindy and I went with the rest of the guests to a reception in our honour. The conversation struck me as boring, and I wanted to get moving.

'Come my dear,' I addressed her, 'They are waiting for us.'

'As guest of honour likely,' she answered back, 'Will I see your brother again? He seems nice and polite, though I think he is mistaken to compare me to a Draconian forest. I'm just plain ol' Cindihan.'

'Don't forget you are Cindihan *Huer*, and I wouldn't put it past him to pitch a tent in that forest and harbour your front,' I sneered, pausing.

And I continued, 'That pleasure is mine, and mine alone, yeah? He may be charming and well-endowed in the brain cycle, but I fear what will come of it.'

She sighed, not understanding the full rivalry between us.

'Okay, Elias, but it couldn't have been *that* bad between you. I mean, you are brothers. I didn't even have any siblings to squabble with! That pleasure was with other people who clashed with me.'

I knew where she was going on this conversational trail, and I wanted desperately to pitch a signpost that said, 'STOP!' Her problems should have remained back in Anarchia. Not in a delicate place like this.

So, I suddenly got firm with her. 'Look, you may not have grown up with a brother, per se, but I know mine very well. He's been influenced by books and now Dracos. Can you imagine such a person with that kind of knowledge?'

'Yes,' she snapped, 'A person who has the gumption to better himself.'

'What can be more better than being the son of a scientist?'

She huffed in her place, and considered the standpoint. 'Maybe science isn't for him.'

I crawled back into my arena, huffing away. 'That is what *he* said. Years ago.'

'Well, a man should know his actions, then,' she went toward the vehicle; I followed her. I did not see Silage, nor the Kanes, and figured they'd entrap us at the reception. Well, not meaning *entrap*, but I wouldn't put it past Silage. The Kane brothers grew up well for *normal* gentlemen, and became so. Silage, well, that was another incident altogether.

The evening lasted with rambunctious fervour and excitement at the fore.

They certainly knew how to party in the 25th century, and I wondered if the Januard entity will make a comeback in the heavens. It twirled around, making appearances all over the Earth, and possibly other planets in the star system. I wondered how others celebrated the delight. We still didn't know what it was, nor did we bother to examine it. As a newly formed society, we couldn't afford luxuries like astronomy yet, but we were getting to the point, where we were able to do so.

I arrived with Cindy, and Pemur waited for us, providing good support. I allowed them a few dances together, before I eventually wanted to cut in. It was nice to be able to dance with her, alone and for myself.

The cake arrived, but nothing popped out of it. Not like centuries earlier, when a special someone would do a greeting by 'popping out' of the cake. If I knew Silage, I could imagine, what or even who, he'd want out of his cake. I sighed at the thought, as a slice was given to me by Cindy. Just an ordinary chocolate chip flavoured cake, with fantastic decorations and swizzling sparklers on top.

The Kanes danced with various women of the crowd. They enjoyed the company and loved the opportunity to mingle with them. I could not fathom what Draconian women were like, but it was more pleasant to be with one's own. Someone in the crowd wanted the synth-band to play something more organic, from the old days. It was surprising, and not, to discover it was Silage himself, who requested some more Celtic-style tunes.

I thought it was probably a reflection of his knowledge, probably a reflection upon my Cindy, with whom he wanted to dance. And I let him, just. I allowed him one dance with her. You couldn't accuse me of being *unfair*.

I didn't mind them talking, but his newly formed attractiveness made him dangerous. They shook their bodies to the tunes Silage requested. He loved the smooth melodies, and he didn't care if they were first performed on parchment paper over a millennia ago. When the medley ended, and we were back to 'normal' music, I gladly took over.

'Fine dancing, Cindihan,' Silage commented. 'I appreciate being able to express myself in this antiseptic century.'

Not undeterred by his quaint comment, I was about to speak, before another lady rushed in to grab Silage for another dance. He was swiftly taken away by her and the friends who accompanied her. And I thought it was *my* night! I stood there in shock; then, Cindy took me away from all that. She had another dance with me, swaying to and fro the two-toned slow dance music that uttered upon the stereo loudspeakers.

'It is your night, Elias,' she conferred to me.

'Well, cannot be too careful here,' I overheard more contemporary music in the limelight.

I watched Silage and his female crowd dancing. I took Cindy with me to the window, where I spotted revellers carrying on the festivities outside. It became twilight, and some of the guests already had moved on. I had my Cindy now, and we kissed by that window. I sighed, and thought about the upcoming night. *Just her and myself.* It was paradise thinking about it.

Lt Busdon was dancing with someone when he came over and congratulated me on my success.

'Sorry I didn't get a chance to talk to you,' he said, 'Your brother surely takes the command post, doesn't he?'

'He certainly does,' I droned on, wondering what Silage was up to now. I glanced at a small crowd, and he was in the centre of it. *Figures.*

Busdon saw my reaction, and put his hand on my shoulder. 'I wouldn't worry about it. I saw you and Cindy on my ship. Both of you were keen on one another then; probably went on a harrowing adventure together, when I picked you up. You will not suffer him long.'

No, I won't, I said to myself, but outwardly declared, 'He's no fool, but I wouldn't put it past him... to... to,' my face buckled with slight anger, 'I know he's been away for some time, but he's already the ladies man. And I don't want him near…'

I desperately tried to conceal my current feelings after seeing Silage.

'Hey, hold the thought,' Busdon took me aside. 'I know you love Cindy, and seeing you wandering the deserts of Anarchia proved that love. You said you found her out there.

'People out here are not fools, either. They look like they know what they're doing. So does your Cindy.'

He walked away, leaving me in the dark corner. I suddenly lost track of Cindy. *Where was she?* Ah, I saw her dancing with Pemur again, when they stepped my way. I felt a bit better, knowing she was in good hands, and those hands will not a-wander off.

She asked, 'You alright, Elias? I can get you a drink.'

'Yeah, thanks,' I kissed her, and she went off for that libation.

I was alone with Pemur. 'Are you okay, really?'

I squirmed a bit. 'My brother was taking the fancy out of many women here. I'm just afraid he'll come after Cindy.'

'If you need help,' Pemur offered. 'I know how much she means to you.'
'Thanks.'

I shook his hand, and went toward the dance floor. I met up with Cindy, who had my drink. I swilled it down quickly, before another lady took the glass from me to put it down. Then a swarm of dancers surrounded us and we were encircled by them. They drove us to the middle of the room, where a circular computer terminal was brought out. It came to life, twinkling with those familiar lights and proceeded with thanksgivings toward us. In an odd manner, the machine provided a playful, yet mischievously drawn-out voice. Monochrome as it sounded, it gave the moment personality.

'We thus impart to you Elias and Cindihan Huer, as guests of honour of this elaborate engagement, many years of happiness. May your sparks fly further toward the next star-field. May you never run into an interplanetary mess of asteroids, and that your bonding is as secure as a tightened Earthen envelope of yore.'

The guests applauded, and I was amused at the archaic bit at the end.

I'd bet Cindy's purse strings it was Silage who conjured up those wishing-well sentiments to us. *Well, it was a nice gesture, if it was him.* Never could I think that my brother to be so thoughtful.

The party was primarily over and the guests started to vacate toward their vehicles for an endless night. My folks would have been proud of all this and Cindy herself. I believe I married well. At least I did, but what about Silage? Who will he choose as his bride, or brides, if I recalled Draconian culture properly.

Pemur, Cindy, and I went to our vehicle to settle down for the night. The Kanes left with some women from the party, and Silage was still with us. It seemed like an all-round family affair and I was glad to have him over.

'I wish you all the best, Brother Elias,' he said.

I appreciated his love, but that 'brother' bit had to go. 'Thank you, just Elias would be way better.'

'Yes, but you are my brother. You deign to call me Silage.'

He was right. I did call him Silage, and will for all time.

'I'm not a monk, you know,' I smiled at him.

'I know. Not with the woman you're carrying around,' he smiled back, pointing and wishing he could be… I thought not on the subject, and let him in with us. As a family and friend (in Pemur's case), we went out for drinks, before setting off toward a new day. The stars shone in their brightest glory and it was a clear night.

I wished I had a telescope with me, so I can show off my boring self to Silage, to get him away from me. But who knew that Silage would be interested in stargazing too? I never did; probably something he picked up on Dracos.

He noticed my longing hand gestures and muttered, 'What do you think the ancient Earth cultures lived by?'

I asked innocently, 'By what?'

Silage pointed upwards. 'That is what fate, power and glory are based on. It is all in the stars. Fascinating isn't it, when you do not have any other explanation? Science may be our light today, but no one knew about it back then. Belief in the heavens were a sure sign of human development. Religion was a strong force in the universe. Even though the stars eventually got charted, it was much later, in *your* sphere of study.'

He walked off, leaving me to drink in further wonderment. I looked up and glanced at a few more organised star features. I wondered about the Januard and if it were to make another appearance. It probably did, in some other part of Earth. I could sense the celebrations arising and the onset of drunkenness to offset a good time. I stood close by Cindy, who watched me, knowing what I was really after. We stood outside in silence, as we observed the experience of a great mystery.

CHAPTER IV

We had a honeymoon on the outskirts of Aurora Star, a faraway district of New Chicago. Sequestered for fun and games, it was with plenty of leisure time in space; your own space. Overall it was enjoyable, and Cindy and I loved it. I got to know her better, and I thought she was the betterment of the girl I saw, floating around in mere existence around the region of Anarchia. I thought we'd both come along since then.

We walked along a moonlit path in the outer junction, and looked at the stars. It seemed like a past-time I would enjoy for life's duration. Cindy looked on with me and got romantic, kissing me. It made me think I should have brought a telescope with me, or something, knowing I would admire the heavens. *But phoo, I didn't.* I thought to buy one in the local area, a portable something for just in case. It pained me to watch myself struggle against the forces of nature.

Cindy seemed like she was struggling within herself. She started to look around, slightly panicked. Her demeanour was uncomfortable by this point, and I grew concerned about her.

'What's wrong, my little Cindihan?'

'I don't know,' she answered, still looking around her. 'I thought I saw something or someone I once knew.'

I enquired, 'A friend?'

'No, just someone I thought I saw in Anarchia. I didn't think they would come out this way. I thought they'd all stay put where they were. They were like that, you know,' Cindy explained.

'Okay,' I tugged her sleeve. 'Let's go, quickly.'

We raced away from the small haven we'd created for ourselves, and went along a more public promenade. It was full of shops and food courts, with hundreds of people milling around, talking, getting to know one another. I wanted to get to know Cindy, but not this way. And certainly not in a hurry, as we were.

I had an idea. 'You want something to eat? Might calm your nerves.'

'Yeah, I'd like that,' she accepted and took my hand.

We walked along to see what lovely things were available. Cindy looked around, all eyes, and she believed her pursuer was gone. Her relaxed composure was welcome at this moment in time.

She settled down at a table with me, as I perused the menu somewhat.

'I miss your brother. He seemed so interesting,' she commented.

'Well,' I had to agree with her on this. 'Interesting, yes. Polite, yes. But what I do not like is what all that archaic knowledge will bring him. I mean, it is good to read history and the like, but he took it so seriously. As a boy, I saw him read the books, I heard him practising spells. My oh my, what will all that lead to, I wonder? He even looked different, sort of a lady-killer man, so to speak.'

'He seemed quite pleasurable to me, at least in sight. I liked him.'

'You would. Many women fall for his sort,' I sat dismayed. 'I thought when he was with you that you would, ummm....'

'Go for him? After what we went through, Elias!'

'I know, I know,' I grunted. 'Picked anything yet?'

'Small vanilla ice cream and some tea.'

'Okay, I'll return soon.'

I got up and left her to place the order at the stand-alone kiosk. I looked around me and after pressing some buttons, I checked to see how my wife was doing. She seemed okay, at a short distance, but you never could tell with these things. I then came back as promised, holding the receipt.

'See,' I said, holding her hand, 'That wasn't so bad, now was it?'

'No, I guess,' she hung her head in shame.

Suddenly, a woman in a black overcoat with beige trousers, and curly light coloured hair soon came into view. She wasn't sure where she was going, but looked like she had intent. I was wondering why she was here. I hesitated and hung my head down for protection, just for the time being. She came along, tittering and asking around for something. I was so desperate to put an end to the mania when she approached our table.

'Ah, there you are Cindihan,' the lady said. 'I thought it was you.'

'Oh, hi,' Cindy responded plainly.

'It's been a long time, how've you been?'

'Fine. This is my husband, Elias Huer. I'd just gotten married and we're on our honeymoon.'

I gave a slight 'hello' wave to her. 'And you are?'

'I'm sorry, I'm Kendra Soonali. I thought I recognised you earlier, but I was unsure. I didn't want to approach to quickly,' the lady continued.

'That's okay,' Cindy offered, 'Do you wish to have something?'

'No, I've got to get on. I've a lot of shopping to do, and things to get for my husband,' Kendra said.

I piped up, 'Are you still in Anarchia?'

'No, no,' she answered, 'We're living in the Del-Rae section of the Inner City. It's really nice and our home is large and lavish. Right by a marina, so we can float a boat, if we want.'

I was curious about this, so I continued, 'Are just you and your husband living there?'

'Yes,' Kendra answered. 'Our only child is in the Directorate, working bur-eaucratically.'

'Ah,' I exhaled, as the orders came in.

'I'll excuse myself now,' Kendra replied, 'You take care, and congratulations.'

'Thank you,' Cindy waved back.

The woman left us to our food.

I thought about the conversation, sipping on my cool soda. 'Bit of a drag, no?'

'Eh, it's alright. She's fine, but I did not expect to see her long.'

'Why?'

'She has her own things going on, and so do we.'

'That's a good answer.'

We left when we finished and took a long walk back to our accommodation. We had another few days to go, when we decided to go fishing, which led to swimming, and played various things like tennis, racquet ball, and the like. We had enormous fun and it allowed bonding between us. The best bit was that it was mostly needed, in case we do anything else together. Maybe flying. *Maybe if I could get her to go on missions with me...*

Our time in Aurora Star came to a quick end, lasting a mere week, but it was a good refreshment. I noticed a blistering sunburn, near the end of the honeymoon. Cindy thought it was a tan, and said I looked good in it. I reckoned I looked like an overcooked lobster.

Her way of seeing things was better, as she thought very highly of me. I wondered what Silage would say about this bodily anomaly. Probably he'd shake my hand, stating I looked wonderfully sun-kissed. Nothing like a sun-kissed scientist, I guess. Still, I thought about him, and his bronze-aged look. *Eh, to each his own, but if only in moderation.*

My time with Cindy was good too, and just as exploratory. She revelled in the hype of being with someone, since it was a condition of life she was not used to. It was nice to share one's life with her, and someone to call family, as opposed to a brother who was on another world; so distant, with a mind even farther. She came to me with last-moment anxieties, which I calmed her down from. It was good to talk about things and her earlier times in Anarchia. The information gained though wasn't discussed further, as she was eager to move away from it all, and my patience allowed her to do so. I loved her with all my heart, and wanted this life to work out for *her*.

My brother, Silage, was another matter I needed to consider. As we were now old enough to be called 'adults', and make our own paths in life, I wondered about him. I had not seen him since the wedding. He was still on Dracos, so no love there. Though, I reflected at his near-rebellious state of being, with those history books (specifically the one on Irish lore), his magic tricks, and his will to make himself planet-bound elsewhere. It was sad, because as he was a twin, we usually stuck together. Unfortunately for me, we did not. We were always at odds from the beginning and it was at the beginning that the weirdness flowed. Small messages from Dracos came trickling in, a sort of postcard message, *'Hi brother, doing great, hope you and Cindy are well. Love, Silas'*; not great clangers of information. It was more like he spent his time imbibing in the culture and recreations of Dracos. A 'wish you were here' type of existence.

I was glad to see he was happy in his new life; perhaps he found a Draconian beauty for himself, as I found Cindy. Yet, for all he was worth, he was *still* Silage to me, and it was a name I would see later fulfilled.

Upon my return, Cindy and I went to the family home I grew up in on Jossi Hill Road, which I inherited upon my father's death. As long as I kept up the payments and other solemnities, I was welcome to live there, and start anew. I felt it would do for now, and Dad's insurance payout was a big help to me. The place didn't look any different. We had to rearrange some things to fit our needs, as we were only two people and no longer a family of four.

The ghosts of the past crawled up to me and memories flashed like a lightning bolt. I remember all the times we had together, Mother, Dad, Silage and me. It haunted me terribly to see it all gone, and I am left with its consequence: the family homestead. All that was in it was for Cindy and I to make do with *now*. I did some organising around the house, closing doors to some rooms and making space for us in another. The lab was still intact, with all Dad's accoutrements of science. I pondered hard on how much he wanted me to take over, to make him proud of future achievements.

Well, I felt I had bad news for him. My future achievement lay in flying around space, to see if there was anything worth flying around about. I knew there was something out there. I knew there was more to Earth than New Chicago, or any other city prefixed with the word *New* in their title!

There had to be a reason why there is a star out there we keep seeing every year, or so, depending on where on Earth you lived. I wanted so badly to go out there and find the source of all my wonderment.

There was always a reason for things. Even in science, all experimentation leads to logical conclusions. *God, I'm sounding like Dad!*

I crashed on the sofa, exhausted, and rubbing my face.

Cindy went up to me, and lightly touched my forehead. 'You okay, darling?'

'Yeah,' I assured her, giving her a kiss, 'Thanks for asking. How about you?'

'Fine. I appreciated Aurora Star. It was a nice place to visit.' She made a quick pause. 'Are you going to fly out to the stars, like you wanted?'

I mumbled aloud. 'Yeah, I want to fly out.' I stopped myself to consider her comment about the honeymoon.

My mind was no longer there. *A nice place*, she called it. One among many. One of the newly refurbished resorts and recreation hot-spots of old Earth, just newly named. *Vegas was another.* I wasn't in the mood now to be frivolous with precious commodities, like relaxation. My dream of being a pilot-explorer was still on my mind. What I wanted to do with my life was my concern. I know my folks were more keen on me following Dad's footsteps into the sciences, but I wanted to have fun. I couldn't wait to go on; the pure joy of space flight was nurtured from the books I'd read as a child. Those old rudimentary science books were all it took for me to want to explore the stars and our place within their masked fore. It was a mystery worth the trip, unlike cultural mysteries, which lounged in human imagination.

Later, after settling in together, Pemur Oppenmach came to visit. He figured in my life more frequently, and acted like a surrogate father to me. I found it odd that *he* of all people would come to my aid. Not that I needed much; I was a fully-grown man. Okay, I was a *young*, fully-grown man, yet to discover the widest possibilities with Cindy, on Earth or in space. I did appreciate his mother-hen approach to me. It felt like a good substitution, a support, if you will. Yet, with him and Cindy in my court, I felt like that old Irish King standing tall in his realm of majestic beauty, his name notwithstanding.

I welcomed him inside, and he sat on the sofa.

After all the silly banter about our trip was ended, he asked, 'Are you two ready for the next push of your lives?'

Pemur and I discussed my interest in helping out with the flight programs offered, and the possibility of exploring space. *That* was something I really wanted to do.

'I think so,' I nodded confidently, pointing onward. 'I am looking forward to seeing the Earth from *out there*.'

'I'll see that you do get 'out there', if we can help it,' he said, 'I'll assign Cindy as your co-pilot, and even your ambuquad, Twiki can help out. I'll send out feelers to the Soleil Flying Academy and happily sponsor you. We can never get enough pilots for scouting or defence.'

'No you can't, and Cindy would make a great co-pilot, won't you, dear?'

She smirked and put an embarrassed face on.

'Ah, she's shy,' Pemur grinned. 'It's nothing to shy away from, girl. You will be doing us a great service. For the planet.'

'Thanks for your confidence in me, sir,' Cindy shook his hand.

'You needn't get so formal, Cindihan,' he responded, full name and all.

'Nah, I'm like that,' she went on, trying to impress and mind the manners.

He followed, 'Is that what they taught you in Anarchia?'

'Well,' she made a face, 'It's a survivalist game out there, and sometimes to survive, you have to talk straight; I treat you as someone of importance.'

'You needn't be straight with me,' Pemur grinned. 'But I accept your way of things.'

'I know, but,' she dwindled on in thought, then gave up. 'Thank you.'

Pemur then laid a small object on the table. Cindy and I watched him as he took out a filled pipette, and applied some water drops onto the item.

'This is your father's legacy, or part of it,' he stated, 'He worked on it when he died, and wanted to have a celebratory send-off. I thought this occasion would warrant it.'

The object transformed into a stunning and stylish dinner service. I figured it was probably what Master Barkhor would muster, if he had the technology we got. If he had it, the Outer region would rival New Chicago, and it would be just as masterful.

The table became magically ornate, like an antique, complete with candle-lights, and edible treats; a full course meal, without the take-away prices or quickened quality. I figured Silage would appreciate the immediacy of the effect.

'Dinner is served,' Pemur announced, taking his place at the table, but not sitting down.

Cindy and I were stunned. I asked, 'This is for us?'

'Yep. Before he passed, your father wanted you to have the best, in case you found someone special in your life, or it could be used as a memorial to him, in appreciation of his life and work. He didn't live long to see it, but thought it would make a great gift in any case.'

We all sat at the table to a luxurious banquet. *A great gift. Thanks, Dad.* I wondered about the long hours he spent at the lab, at Mother's and our expense. It was certainly thoughtful of him, us not knowing what he was up to in that space of his. I reckoned it was one of his pet projects, like when you wrote a will in the old days, but better. Here, the deceased gave you a treat, as well as a will. Of course, it was a peculiarity of Dad's, and I sincerely doubted others would follow a death with a fantastic meal, made up by the deceased himself.

We started eating and enjoying the lovely food laid out for us, when Pemur quickly got up.

'Oh, I almost forgot.'

I was curious. 'What?'

'Your drone, Twiki,' Pemur revealed. 'He's been missing you and eagerly awaits to see you again.'

Twiki! Oh, how I missed him. Truthfully, recent events hampered my memory of him, but it would be great to see the little fellow again. This time, *for good.*

CHAPTER V

Dinner obviously would not be complete unless Twiki was there, complimenting the scenery. The little drone of my youth came up to me, waddling and beading. His stout shape was well-buffed and shiny, like a utensil out of an old dishwasher. The face looked happy, if you were to call it that. Although his features were stationary, the expressions danced to jigs that even Silage couldn't do.

He spoke in the colloquial programming that I remembered. 'How ya doin', kid?'

'Gosh, I missed you so much,' I cried excitedly, hugging him.

'Likewise,' the drone said, looking at Cindy. 'Who's the bird?'

Ah, he didn't know I'd married. It had been a fair time since I last saw Twiki. I found out from Pemur he'd been relocated to the Directorate and working with him since Dad died. Other lab paraphernalia, except what was at home, was held back until my return. It was all fated to be mine, anyway, as if I'd amassed a great fortune. I was the one who was the most likely to use what was in there. Silage certainly would not. He was *elsewhere*; his mind, well I'd leave that for now.

'This is my wife, Cindihan Huer,' I proudly introduced. 'Cindy, this is my lovable little friend, Twiki. We'd known each other from childhood.'

The clever wit came through from her. 'Whose?'

I put my hand to my face in embarrassment and cried, 'Mine, silly!'

She giggled, as Twiki nearly fell back in shock. 'Your wife? I hadn't realised the time passing. Looks like you've grown up some, Elias.'

'I had,' I smiled, kissing her.

Cindy went up to the quad, holding his mechanical hand. 'Hi, Twiki. It's an
honour to meet you.'

'Awwh, shucks,' he blushed in a robotic manner.

'I'm not just saying that,' she continued, 'It is good to meet my husband's
old friends.'

Twiki, still blushing, moved his hand in a motion suggesting, 'Ah, don't
mention it.'

'Guess what?' I interjected, 'I might get to pursue my dream of flying.'

The quad showed excessive happiness. 'Can I be your co-pilot? I can be
useful with the on-board ship systems and computers.'

'Cindy will be my co-pilot,' I revealed, 'But you can still help out with the
systems, and piloting, if she gets tired. She's only human, you know.'

'You do that, Twiki,' Pemur entered the conversation. 'Let's eat now, there is
more later.'

We helped ourselves to the gourmet-style food in the silver-plated dish
ware. Dad wasn't great at cooking; he left that to the women. Yet, what he
did try for a meal turned out to be quite good.

Steak, potatoes, side of vegetables, wine and a fruit sorbet had gone well together. It was actually delicious, and it had been awhile since I last ate like *this*.

'Actually, I programmed the food recipe into your father's invention. That's why it is so good,' Pemur revealed.

I smiled, as I finished my meal and turned away toward the window. The stars were getting ready to shine a show for us, as dusk was settling in. The view from the room made me yearn for it all the more. Cindy saw me and raced by my side.

She observed, 'You like looking out windows, don't you, Elias?'

'I do. I like to know what's out there,' I told her.

'Don't blame you really. I've made an art form of it. I lived in the un-known. Unknown to most, anyway.'

We finished the night and the moon swept its light upon the distant bal-conies of the bridges and buildings of New Chicago.

The stars and entwined galaxies shown themselves to many an interested, peering telescope, which you could see in the night air.

* * * * * *

Later on, I was training for flight at the Caprix One station. It wasn't really so difficult, but I had to get used to gravicentric forces which will envelope me within my ship. The ship itself was the *Scout-600*, was a multi-passenger vehicle, with a prostylene finish and a gearbox. It would be some time before I get into a real Scout ship, as the training would persist for six months to a year in order to gravitate the forces upon my person. Cindy was the other passenger in the vehicle. She initially enjoyed being in the cockpit, helping me out. It was great to see her skill go into full bloom, as I saw so much potential in her when I took her away from Anarchia. However, something did go wrong, and she twittered a little in her seat.

'I'm okay,' she dismissed the weakness.

Any weakness would get her off the ship, but she composed herself gradually into the co-pilot she was meant to be. *With me.* Twiki wasn't with us at this point, because drones could go in a ship at any time and not get physically sick like we do. Their equipment was meant for flight, and earlier models and tinkerings of past drones were used, somewhat, to explore. The problem was in getting them to return. Right now, it was us who had to get used to the ongoings of the ship.

However, when we did unite eventually, Twiki had a whale of a time, down to its tail tip. We tried a flight simulation together. Everything was in order, and Cindy perused the scanner in front of her.

Pemur was with us too, but on the outside. He counted down, 'Three, two, one.'

Whoosh! Twiki, Cindy and I sailed into the heavens, or what *looked* like the heavens, from our standpoint. The simulator was contained in a section of the training grounds, with Pemur and Lt Busdon watching over us. They wanted to be certain we wouldn't get into mischief. I had my hand on the controls, as Twiki this time read the console in front of him. He and Cindy were good in their respective stations and I was pleased to have them on board. With Cindy, it would be even better, when we can do more *organic* things together, as Twiki could take the helm itself during a sleep-span.

'The simulator checks out a-okay, boss,' Twiki announced.

I muttered, 'Good, we don't want to be on the wrong flight path, do we?'

I had Twiki take control for a bit, while Cindy and I monitored for bumps and bruises along the way. The simulation monitor displayed a colourful set of lights at this point.

Cindy called out, 'What's that?'

'It's showing the time lapse of our flight. We are now 'entering' another sector. Peter-one-two,' I counted.

'Wow, imagine what space itself will be like,' Cindy aired, as she floated about in a dream-state, fighting her 'weakness'.

'Yeah,' I said, 'We're just touching the edge of our atmosphere. Anything can go wrong.'

The simulator bumped and steered, as we 'travelled' within our fake-space.

It was a good run, and this training would come in handy for when we really do some serious space travel. Twiki carried on steering, but we headed into a small cloud of pretend emission dust, before gaining control of our axis point.

'Sorry,' he said.

'As a simulator, it's very realistic. Nothing like an amusement park ride at all,' Cindy noted. 'This is better.'

'It's not like you've been to any amusement parks lately, have you?' I decided to take the controls and give Twiki a break. 'We're heading for Peter niner-six-one-two. Just exiting our system, tracking where we've been.'

Cindy asked, 'When will we leave our system?'

'We won't,' Twiki explained. 'It's just made to look like we're leaving. We cannot deviate beyond our programmable flight path.'

I smirked, as Cindy faced a 'duh' moment in time. Space flight was nothing to sniff at, and it was a doozy to deal with. With vectors, control panels, petra trajectories, and more items to come across with, all sorts of things could happen. But, nothing could and nothing did, because it was, after all, a simulator!

Soon, our ride came to a close. At least it was a smooth one. The more bumpy, jarring types were in the advanced classes. The three of us exited the large-scale simulator, with Pemur and Busdon approaching us.

'That's good fancy work you put out there, Elias,' Busdon complimented me. 'Are you ready for further g-forces upon your person, because they will be intense. You may have to wear something extra that will help you cope with them.'

'I think I'd like to try more simulations to get the feel of them,' I smiled. 'It was okay so far, though.' I looked at Cindy. 'You alright? You look haggard.'

'I guess it wore me out some. It's been okay with you, Elias,' she held my arm, and laid her head on it.

'I think you two should reset yourselves for the next time, tomorrow, 0900,' Busdon said.

He then took out a small box and gave it to me. 'This is for you, Cadet Huer.'

I found it weird that I was addressed as *Cadet* Huer. I opened the small box he gave me, and a gold pin with wings was nestled within the cotton wool inside.

'It's beautiful,' I gleamed, putting the pin on my lapel.

'Here's to your first flight simulation. May there be many more, with real flights too,' Pemur congratulated me.

I accepted the honour. Cindy applauded and gave me a hug. Twiki beaded like there was no tomorrow.

'You're on your way, Elias,' she said, 'This is what you'd been after. Those old laboratories can wait.'

'They sure can,' I replied.

We walked away from the simulator into a nearby canteen, where we were toasted and treated to drinks. The newly awarded pin was very encouraging, and I was pleased to see myself supported into newfound fame. Well, it wasn't fame as such, but I did feel a bit more popular than I cared to imagine. However, that wasn't all Pemur had in store for me. There was another surprise, which we found out much later in the day.

CHAPTER VI

After the lovely refreshments and Busdon excused himself, we went to Pemur's office in the Directorate Building. Twiki beaded happily; Pemur had something important to share with him. He took out a circular box, with a silver coloured twine ribbon. I looked on with Cindy, and wondered what could Pemur have. It seemed strange that all this gift giving was overwhelming me a bit. I liked surprises, somewhat, but never would I have thought my endeavours would be so fruitfully rewarded. I vaguely recalled the conversation I had with Dad about the hooks on Twiki's chest area. The box seemed the correct size and shape to go on them.

Pemur was about to reveal the contents of the box. 'Ready guys?'

'Guess so,' I said casually.

Twiki wanted a hand in helping Pemur with the box, so he let the drone untie the ribbon. The knot was already loosened, and now it was just a pull-off. The ribbon came off the box and inside was a beautiful and delicate piece of technological exquisiteness I'd ever seen. My eyes flew wide open, revealing an intense blue I never exhibited before. A cascade of Christmas lights, confined within the holding box itself, lit up and a friendly voice stirred awake, as if it were refreshed from an afternoon nap.

'Hello,' the unit spoke suddenly.

I nearly jumped out of my skin. Cindy stared at it, as if it were a 'toy', with lights, rotary bits and all.

Pemur addressed the quad. 'Twiki, this is Dr Theopolis, your computer-driven counterpart.'

Twiki looked expectant, as Pemur took the unit and carefully put it on those hooks I wondered about for all these years. The pair looked complete, and Twiki had a new friend, even though the friend was *more* sophisticated than the quad himself.

'Oh boy, I feel complete now,' Twiki beaded excitedly.

Now I knew how it felt when I met Cindy in Anarchia.

Pemur smiled and knelt down to the quad. 'This is a superific superior machine you've got on, Twiki, so please do not be careless with it.'

'I won't,' he promised.

'And you, too, Elias,' Pemur warned, pointed his finger at me.

'I will be careful,' I promised, 'It will be like putting Christmas lights on the tree!'

Pemur scoffed away; the newly robotic unit tried to master the hilarity, but it went unnoticed. *Typical machinery; that was all these hob-nob devices were. Machines!* Yet, my eyes lit up with a passion I never felt before. The little device would be a boon to most things, and to think that his counterparts were on the Computer Council!

I was really impressed and honoured to have one of these systems for my own use. The lights started to scramble into more accessible English, overriding the multitude of binary codes and logic, programmed within the unit.

'It is nice to meet with you all,' Theopolis said, coolly, with precise demeanour. 'You are Dr Huer's son, Elias Jr, correct?'

'I am,' I stated. Gosh, this was fascinating, and the memories just flooded into the bathwater. 'And this is my wife, Cindy.'

Cindy got close to the unit with equal interest. 'How do you do? I think it would be most difficult to see you as a mere computer. You seem more intricate than I remember anything metallic being.'

'I am, much to the fascination of your fellow humans. Elias, Sr had programmed me before he died. I was one of the many things that he worked on. I am sorry for your loss; no machine confined within a box of twinkling lights could imagine the vastness of the human spirit.'

'Thank you, Theo,' I imparted, 'Can I call you Theo?'

'You may. We are friends, no?'

'Friendship grows beyond attachment,' Pemur said.

'I trust you will accompany us, being on Twiki all the time,' Cindy assumed.

'Yes,' Theo replied, 'We are two units in a pod, so to speak. When the moon is blue and the sky rises, I shall be here at your side.'

'I wasn't expecting convoluted poetry from a box,' I noted.

'Convoluted or not,' Theo continued, 'I am your drone's attachment. I can help you in many ways, at least in an advisory capacity. After all, I am only a clock-shaped box full of Christmas lights.'

Ha-ha, so he got my joke.

Pemur smiled, 'You certainly have a way with words, Elias.'

'Let's just say, it was the best description I could come up with,' I laughed.

'Oh brother,' Twiki uttered.

Cindy giggled. I gave her a kiss. It was getting late, and we decided to meet for the training flight in the morning.

* * * * *

Mornings had a bad habit of sneaking up on you when you don't know it. Or do know it, if you're an insomniac. The netted curtains wafted gently in the breeze, as the sun lit up the sky once again. I was to alight in space, which was something to look forward to, one day. Still a *pretend* flight was better than nothing at all, and equally fun, but without the danger particles involved.

Twiki and Theo were currently housed in the laboratory of our home, where Dad worked. They stood still, and switched off like a domestic light. When you activated them, they were as lively as a gift-bearing party-goer. And not to mention the lights! They would *alone* make a good gift, which even has the audacity to talk back to you!

Ah, it was something to be cherished, and not only that, it was something (or someone), I eagerly looked forward to working with.

I got up, and nudged Cindy awake.

She mumbled, 'That you, Elias?'

'Who else would it be, but me?'

She looked up and smiled at me.

We got dressed, ate something, and switched on Twiki and Theo. We reported back at the simulator deck at Caprix One. Busdon was waiting there with eager eyes, and fitness to match.

I expected someone else, in addition. 'Where's Pemur?'

'He'll be along now,' he answered, 'Probably getting his socks wrong or something.'

We had a quick giggle over it, when I was taken back to the simulator for another round of fake flight. I had to wear a different and more robust flight suit, with an inner lining to combat the strong forces, as did Cindy. The levels would be more intense this time, in this upcoming bout of flight. Lucky Twiki and Theo came as they were, because they didn't need all the protective gear like we did. 'Twas a shame we weren't robots... *or were we?* Like the budding scientist I was, I thought about this from time to time, but never found a satisfactory answer. I didn't need to, because I was allowed passion and reason to co-mingle together, with reason taking the lead. Yet, you couldn't underestimate passion.

'This time I've prepared the rig to take you beyond the range you're used to. It would be a test of endurance and utmost strength. I'm willing to send you off; I hope you are ready for it, Elias.'

'Glory be, if I didn't know a coon-hound from a starship,' I horsed about with him, and boarded the ship with Cindy, Twiki and Theo. 'Thank you for your help, Lt.'

'No problem,' Busdon said.

We strapped in for the ride of our lives, so it seemed. It was awkward for Twiki, with a new load on his chest. I adjusted his straps to account for that.

'Okay, we're ready,' Cindy announced.

'Let's go,' I commanded.

The sensors in the cockpit twinkled, as the underside feeling began.

And there we were, on our 'flight', with a whoosh, a clang, and a boop. The simulator moved quietly at first, as Lt Busdon looked on with glee. He programmed the thing to give us a 'longer' duration, and probably a few surprises. *Who knows?*

We wobbled on track, as the once-blue sky turned into a star-field, aligned with us within an exuberant trajectory. Asteroids passed us, as did a small moon or two. We were blanketed in pure velvet sheen and it looked amazing. The excitement couldn't be left for another day. I showed much glee, and I forgot myself momentarily.

Cindy, of course, had to ask, 'Are we still in our solar system?'

'Duh, yeah,' I snapped, 'We're still in New Chicago, remember. This is all a ruse for us. An ordinary flight patterned T-Neth 500.'

'Oh,' Cindy reclined in the back seat and left the monitoring to Twiki and Theo.

Theo was no more lively than an icicle in a wonderland. 'We are coming up to Mars now, having surpassed your Moon.'

The red planet looked ablaze with energy, but devoid of life, *for now*. Maybe when we are more enlightened in space, we will explore that option, too. We flew past other planets, major and minor, though the latter were moons more than anything else. Even the celebrated Januard entity I recalled from my youth came into view, but it was too fuzzy to determine what it was.

But then something weird happened. We carried along a path that led us to a whirlygig of sight, sound and colour. Probably something the ancient hippies of the 20th century would deeply appreciate. We didn't know what it was, but more stars transformed themselves into what seemed like a passing gate. Once through it, it made you think of old adventures of long ago.

I panicked slightly. 'What's our heading?'

'Peter Roger delta, alpha three-o-nine,' Theo announced, 'We are going through what's called a stargate.'

At this point, I hadn't heard of any star cluster forming into a gate of some kind, but I left it to Theo to check it out.

The colours illuminated around us, and were stunning. It was a challenge to explain another station in life, when yours seemed wanting. It was difficult to believe this was just a simulation, and I became disappointed that it was. I really wanted to make a difference in New Chicago, maybe to better-half myself against Silage. I was really wishing to slog it out for history. But within the safe confines of the simulator jet-thing, we were exploring our hearts out!

CHAPTER VII

And explore we did. Only this time, it wasn't the simulator, and my head hurt. It felt as if something hit me, and I didn't live here anymore. The last thing I remembered was being through a stargate, or what I *thought* was a stargate. Now, I was in a daze, and slowly awoke from the roused sleep. I opened my eyes fully and noticed one of the oddly shaped consoles of the ship had dislodged accidentally. I put it back to its original place, with a heavy groan. I pressed a few buttons to see if anything happened. *Nothing.* The screens let off a digital immersion that sparkled and waved, as if it were the middle of the night and the station conked out to sleep.

Oh boy, and there was Cindy, Twiki and Theo to consider!

'Cindy,' I called, 'Cindy, are you okay?'

A rustle of belt wires spread voluminously in one corner. 'Elias?'

'Cindy,' I repeated her name like a song, and bolted to free her from the technological nightmare we were in at the moment.

'Elias, what happened?'

'I don't know,' I looked around me. 'I don't know.'

Something was missing. I looked for the drone and his conscience. They were gone. I couldn't help but wonder about them, being such sophisticated pieces of machinery, becoming lost in a confined space. *They had to be here!* Yet, they were not, and I wondered if they were really machinery; calling them equipment would be a dastardly insult. They were just as technical as the ship, but they were more than that.

They were friends, and pretty darn good ones too. Both of them spoke intelligibly, and right now, their voices were sorely needed to soothe this major calamity. Especially Theo. It seemed like his bolts always tuned in on time.

'Twiki,' I called out again, and panicked, not seeing him. Theo was in no better presence, either, being attached to him.

Cindy moaned out of character. 'Twiki's gone? Now what? It's not like you can take him into your back pocket for travel.'

'Quiet, child. It's just us, babe, no drone or circuit breaker attachment. Just us.'

'Now, what do we do?'

Her helplessness was defeating; it certainly wasn't the brash soul I'd met in Anarchia. If she were like this, her fate would have been held back, long ago. Meantime, I tried to get the simulator to get us out of this mess. Without the quad-input, I feared we would be at a great loss. I felt lost without him, too, since Twiki re-emerged into my life after my return to New Chicago.

'I'm hungry,' came the complaints from someone who shouldn't.

'Pipe down,' I shouted, 'I am trying to get us back on course.'

'With what? The monitors are blank and the circuits don't even work.'

'Well, I am trying to be optimistic.'

Cindy folded her arms together. 'Some optimism.'

I disliked her harrumphs, and current attitude to the hostile climate we were in. Well, it wasn't *hostile* as such, but our ship didn't work; nothing on board worked, not even a comm system to call out for help! I also had no idea if we were even still in New Chicago anymore.

If we were not, then, *where the buck where we???* I looked at the hatchway, and thought to open it. It was getting a bit too tight for my liking in here. I adjusted my parameters, and the monitors still ran fuzzy with static. Nothing to go all clingy about, but it was desperate. I was downhearted about what we would find outside, if we *were* outside. Were we outside, still in space or back in New Chicago, as we spill our beans on the floor with Pemur and Busdon laughing themselves silly over our malfunction?

I dismissed all options, as I touched the hatch and grabbed the handle. I made an attempt to escape our current circumstance. Cindy looked at me strangely, but she was a strange sort at the best of times. It came with her upbringing among the primitives, yet it didn't detract from her being a good person overall.

'Elias, are you sure that's wise?'

'We won't know, until we try.'

I struggled to get the door open, the handle proved quite sticky. Not sticky-goo, but just stubborn with intention. *Like Cindy.* The handle started to give a little, as I pushed the barrier open between us and the outer world. I stretched and groaned trying to open the damn thing.

What outer world was anyone's guess, but there was no turning back, once we left our home, or seemed to anyway.

Suddenly, the door finally yielded, and a shot of pale, stale air blew through my hair. I realised we were on reasonable ground, so I left the ship to see what we trounced upon, with Cindy following me. It was a world of some kind. The oxygen flowed through, releasing kind particles into the air, enlivening freshened breath. Grand amounts of trees, foliage and primitive housing lined the outer area with life. It reminded me of one of my Daye ancestors who came across primitive people on a desert island. That must have been some adventure for him! Yet, this was no desert, however. The place we found looked sumptuous and rich with nature's beauty at its finest. A few beings were picking growth from the trees, probably fruits or nuts. They looked like a cross between wing and fur. *A most unique specimen*, I must say.

Now, I would never imagine in my wildest dreams a mix of fur and fowl. The creatures went about their routines, foraging away and talking to one another. Those who stood around were female, and it was apparent they were in charge, making the men of the community go off to find food. Suddenly, I found myself a small shade of a bigger world. A group of those creatures had spotted us and walked over to meet. I held Cindy's simple and glorified self, as I noted someone among the party who looked like their leader.

'Hello,' one of them said, in a very thick subterranean-styled accent. I reckoned she was their leader.

'Hi,' I smiled, introducing myself and the little wire, 'I'm Elias Huer and this is my wife Cindy.'

'My name is Zenix, leader of the Dagji. Welcome to our humble planet.'

'Thank you,' I shook her hand, as her followers were getting restless without her. I looked around the primitive atmosphere, which showed underlying sophistication.

The Dagji leader was just as sophisticated. With long dark hair, small bits of armour surrounding a long flowing tunic, and tawny-shaded eyes, she looked as if she could take on an army, alone! Her clothing overall looked tidy, with a thin layer of dirt to show the lifestyle here.

Cindy asked, 'Where are we?'

'You're in the Xaggadine star system of twelve planets, sixth moon orbit, near our sun,' Zenix explained.

'Without touching it,' one of her aides spoke out.

'Yes, Renelle,' she waved the aides away, giving them tasks, then turning back to us. 'Would you both like some refreshment while you're here?'

'I would, thanks,' I agreed to it, as we were led on a potential adventure.

Zenix asked, 'Where are you two from?'

My pride couldn't be demonstrated more. 'New Chicago. On planet Earth.'

'Ah, the planet that we've heard so much about,' she tittered.

These Dagji certainly knew how to get around!

I pressed, 'And what have you heard?'

'That someone in your finest of history tales had blown the trenches sky high,' she said.

'Well, that's putting it one way,' Cindy sighed.

'Yes, it had been devastating. We've rebuilt somewhat, to a more comfortable level of existence,' I explained. 'We cope with it nicely, but there is an outer region of the area which remains untouched. 'Our society is contained well, and there is much to be said for it. For a people emerging from destruction, I think we've done fine.'

We went through a small passage, where a larger hut was stationed. I was mesmerised by the simplicity of the environment, compared to the twinkling tower blocks of our inner city of New Chicago. Going inside, with such a snug feel, was something I'd never done before. I was used to vastness and large building complexes, as was Cindy, though I thought it was only in her mind. We were offered some fruit and drink, as we sat down on the large cushion laid out for us.

'You certainly make use of your surroundings here,' I commented, looking around the hut.

'It's not bad,' she said, 'I like the warm glow of the place. We made use of the trees, without killing them off, felling them when we have to, creating so much from so little. The system oozes with comfort and heaven help anyone who cares to disturb it. It's beautiful, isn't it?'

'I'd say,' Cindy agreed, taking a bit of what looked like a guava fruit.

'I like to make our people feel at home, since we were from your Earth,' Zenix revealed, in her blissfully tuneful way. 'Once the nuclation happened, we left the planet to find a new home. This was so many years ago; I forgotten any other existence. We weren't around then, but stories crop up, you know. People tell the tales in song and story. That is how we keep alive here.'

'Yeah,' I guessed.

'We decided to go primitive, as other societies had gone on to advanced stages. It is easier, and we've managed well here.'

'I'd agree that you had,' I said, but thinking she wasn't planning to show all her cards at once. She showed too much depth and scrutiny as a leader to do that.

'We've evolved as a species too, taking in wing and fur. Why wear them when you can be them? Isn't evolution great?'

I didn't discuss the matter any further, and chomped on the apple I was eating. It was an interesting hybrid of the sweet and tart; just as healthy too.

'It's all an equal and absent nature of our paths,' Zenix added.

This was getting pretty freaky! I didn't want to think about what was in store for us, but we were willing to stay with the Dagji for the time being. At least until we got our ship fixed.

CHAPTER VIII

We discussed things further, with Zenix's long dark locks swaying in the evening breeze. She looked marvellous, and probably would in the coming moonlight. Cindy looked at her with adversity, thinking the Leader was better than she was. I noted this and came over to my girl to give her a hug of reassurance.

'She may be all flash, but it is but a flash-in-the-pan, as they say,' I told her.

'But who's the flash, really?' Her eyes were wanting for a staring contest.

'You. I married you for who you were and are. I saw a brave girl in a barren world. I didn't like that, so I took you out of it. You wouldn't have survived long there anyway.'

She got petulant with me. 'Oh yeah? I was doing just fine until you turned up.'

I gave a great heaving sigh and left Cindy in her pitiful quadrant. I didn't want to and I would rather let her diffuse the situation herself. *She deserved better, after all.* I didn't like her in Anarchia and definitely wished her bad experiences would be laid to rest where they belonged. I certainly did not regret taking her along with me on this trip and I wanted to give her the time to heal from her past life.

'So as a species, you rose above the world and evolved like us,' I continued the conversation with Zenix.

'You never know what would spring from forged unions,' she dryly commented.

I laughed at that, and thought it would be a good place to set sticks for the time being. We helped out in the community in the meantime and worked with the rest of the Dagji.

A week was spent with them, getting down to basics; this would be something Cindy would understand, thinking about her life in Anarchia. Our bodies got leaner as we worked, and exercise routines were converted into manual labour. It occurred to me that blight wasn't an issue here, as everyone had planted their share and everyone got fulfilled by it when it ripened. Overall, it was a nice take on things.

Zenix had other concerns though, and wished to share them with me.

'There is another group on this planet, the Lesoos, led by a fearsome, gorgon-like woman who is a witch. I don't know her, nor do I know where her tribe comes from. They've had a hold in the area for some time, maybe before we got here even. Who knows? Anyway, the gorgon, for lack of a better name, tried to take our village with sorcery and evil-doings, to fight us for the land.'

Now I felt for her. 'Do they raid your fields?'

'Yes, and our population suffered for it. Maybe a capturing, too, though I cannot imagine why anyone would want one of us.'

After listening to all this, Cindy made a face, recalling, 'That sounds like someone I used to know.'

'Could be from the same tribe, or environment,' Zenix answered. 'Where's the person now?'

'Dead,' Cindy returned the volley. 'I try not to think about it. I can look after myself, and have done for some time.'

'I'm sure you can,' Zenix smiled.

'Cindy was a marvel in Anarchia,' I said, offering hope. 'Believe me.'

The Leader heard something vaguely familiar. 'Anarchia? Isn't that a part of the current Earth that is uninhabitable.'

'There are people there, sketching a bare living together, within malformed buildings. It was alright when I went there, but it would not be a place we'd visit again,' I stated.

'No, I suppose not.' Zenix said thoughtfully. 'So you two met in Anarchia?'

'We did, and I took Cindy out of all that.'

'Wow,' Zenix marvelled.

'My father ordered me to go there. While my brother got to go to Dracos for schooling and culture, I ended up in Anarchia. Great, isn't it?'

'Your father is...,' Zenix tried to guess.

'Dr Elias Huer, Sr. He died recently during my absence.'

'Looks like your brother got the better end.'

'True,' I mused, 'But I've got Cindy. Silage is still single, though who knows what he's up to in that den of his.'

'Is that his name, Silage?'

'It's Silas,' Cindy revealed, 'But as a joke, we refer to him as Silage. If you met him, you'll know why.'

'A slippery pot, I'd say. Well steeped in magic, mythos and history,' I added.

Zenix got excited about him. 'Sounds like a well-rounded fellow.'

'Well-rounded, yes, but it's what he does with those powers is what I'm afraid of,' I said. 'At least I have a woman in marriage.'

'Then it looks as if you had the better end of the bargain, then. Is he still on Dracos?'

'Yeah, probably living the high life of a cad.'

'Why is that?'

'He tried to mess with Cindy a bit at our wedding.'

'I don't think he meant any harm, Elias,' Cindy spoke out.

'But you're mine, not his,' I firmly stated to her.

'That's okay, I like you better anyway,' she got up to wash her hands.

'Getting back to the Lesoos,' I inquired, 'Do you need our help?'

'We can always use an extra hand in things, yes,' Zenix agreed. 'Very nice of you to offer. The other week or so, before you arrived, there were multiple raids on our property. It appeared that they were looking for something or someone. They wrecked the fields quite badly, trying to starve us out, but they didn't take anything. They did it to cover their tracks. Perhaps you can go as sentry for the night. If you want to step in, my team will only be too glad to help you.'

Feeling left out, Cindy interjected as she returned, 'What about me? I want to help.'

'You will remain at camp in the company of my aid, Renelle,' Zenix ordered.

'Oh, I really wanted to help.' Cindy then pouted brusquely.

I took her aside. 'You did your part in Anarchia. Now, it is my turn. You needn't prove nothing to me. I love you.'

'I love you too,' Cindy relented, and gave me an accepting kiss.

'Good, then it is settled.' Zenix got up and shook my hand. 'Any help is better than none.'

This lady spoke sense, and we planned our next move in our sleep. Cindy and I crashed in our assigned tent, as the night-time noises came on. I found it to be eerie and pleasant at the same time. It wasn't that I did this very often. In fact, bunking out was one of the last things I would do.

But on the other hand, I was getting the memories of a lifetime, far more than Dad-in-his-lab ever had. We heard hoppers, choppers, and thorns being pushed aside by mild-mannered mammals who wanted a break in their vicious routines. Soon, I closed my eyes, and fell into a deep sleep.

CHAPTER IX

The next day, I gathered some firewood, when I heard a rustle in the bushes. I thought it was Cindy, but she was helping out back at Zenix's encampment. I looked around me. Nothing on site. So, I kept gathering, acting like the primitive hunter that I was, but was not. I was from New Chicago, and this was a step backward for me. It was no different living in Anarchia; a primitive lifestyle, with futuristic means. It wasn't all grass and dirt out here. Cindy probably had a field day, with her knowing what to do and all that. Yet, it is not as though we went back in time or anything. The gathered wood was mounting in a huge pile, which I put in a wagon. *A few more pieces to go...*

Rustle rustle.

What was that?

I put the final pile on top, and decided to pursue the tree noise, or what sounded like it. I saw some people gathered around, waiting for something, or someone. It wasn't clear as to what it was, and I reckoned it was those in the enemy camp, the Lesoos; the ones Zenix told us about awhile back. I didn't stick around to find out *who* they were, and took my load back to the encampment. Slowly, but with intention.

Soon, the rustling became louder, as I made my way from the wooded area. It looked dark and seedy to me, as the twilight moon was about to spark. I didn't know what came over me, when suddenly, I found myself lassoed by the Lesoos, only without the rope. To be corralled as a prize animal was not what I had in mind; not with *these* people.

'We'll take that,' a prominent leading woman spoke.

One of the tribesmen freed the wagon from me, stripping me of its contents; another bound me like a fly in the net.

Sounds familiar, eh?

The woman, whom I assumed was their leader, asked, 'Who are you and what are you doing here?'

'I am travelling through here, madam,' I answered respectfully, 'And encamping with the Dagji.'

This lady became insistent. 'But who are you?'

'I am Elias Huer of New Chicago,' I finally stated.

'New Chicago, phah,' she spat vehemently, 'Now, state your business here.'

I frowned, and she had the nerve not to identify herself. I thus thought of her as the Leader of the Lesoos.

'I was told to collect wood, ma'am.'

'Do you realise you are on *our* territory?'

'No, I thought these woods belonged to everybody, if they needed it,' I replied.

'They do not,' the Leader searingly gazed at me, 'You will be punished for felling our territory.'

Oh, what's a Huer to do?

'We will keep you here until you tell us who you're with and your stratagems for defence!'

'You'll never get anything from me,' I protested, 'I'm just a wandering traveller.'

'Yeah,' another Lesoos member added, 'Travelling where you don't belong!'

The small crowd gathered upon me, tore off my clothing, and bound me up some more. I was taken to a great pit, which they used to house old discarded texts. The texts looked like... *ugh, they were being eaten by woodworms.* These hearty creatures loved paper of all sorts, and would have made a great form of a recycling plant back home. Only this one accepted humans as refuse, too. A few odd bones and a skull or two lay beneath the entrapped documents. It felt creepy and for once, *I* got scared. The bugs here must have mutated into something more sinister, beyond their abilities. An advanced species of weevils animating from the wreckage of the Big Blast, or nuclation, as Zenix called it.

I was hung upside down for hours, thinking and scheming. Making use of all my abilities, never mind the creatures' down below. Boy, what Dad did for me by sending me to Anarchia was nothing compared to this! At least the Anarchians were somewhat friendly. This lot, *augh!* They were a total dispensation from the common norms of niceties, or at least, good manners. The winds were picking up, as I swayed to and fro above the buckin' pit. It was too gross to bear, and already I was thinking I would not be one of them. Arachnia came to mind, but at least Eri-Cast was reasonable.

I would expect my brother to do something of this sort, if he were on the other team. But we weren't. Lightly adversarial, maybe, but we still remained family. We were brothers, just not for the same cause. And that's what tipped my boat over. It was horrifying to see Silage with Cindy at our wedding. I wondered if Dracos provided good-enough women to fill his appetites. I didn't expect a virgin out of him, either; I figured he'd sown a few wild oats in his time. I'd sown mine, but with a lady I loved. I missed Cindy, and wondered how she was getting on with the Dagji.

I remembered her time with the Anarchians, and recalled how much empowered she was with all the help she provided them, once she was free to do so. This Leader, or whoever she was, proved to be a hurtful challenge for me. Cindy told me a bit about her early years, and how she was manhandled by the grandmother (as she referred to her adversary). Her raising was probably in question, but Cindihan herself was not. I thought about what she said to me over the time we've been together, and the Leader of the Lesoos was not unlike her descriptions of old. At least I was thankful she wasn't here to endure this, otherwise, she'd freak out at the sight of the Leader and run away, fearing the grandmother would rise from the grave.

CHAPTER X

In the meantime, Cindy was helping prepare a meal with Zenix's folk. Her endless skills at survival made her extremely desirable to them. The meal itself consisted of wild boar, hearty green vegetables and ale as a drink. The hunter was rampant in Cindy, as she did much of the cleaning and preparing of the beast. Not that she liked it, mind, but she knew what it meant to live and be well. *Very well.*

Zenix and her aide, Renelle, watched Cindy with awe, as she went along with work delegated to a housewife.

She began with that thick subterranean-styled accent of hers, 'So, you've learned all your skills in the outback of Anarchia?'

'Yes,' Cindy answered, 'It was a long stroll, a difficult haul at times, but I managed it pretty well, I think.'

'You've been really, kind to us,' Renelle admired.

'I'm used to living within a community space. In fact, this place reminds me of Anarchia, and the people in it. You are not unlike them.'

Zenix checked her makeshift timepiece. 'Your husband Elias should have been back by now with that wood I'd asked him to bring over.'

'It has been awhile,' Renelle agreed, 'He should have been here hours ago.'

'Looks like we've got to find him, then.' Zenix got up, adding, 'He may be in trouble, if that rival tribe got to him first. Let's eat now, then we find him.'

They had dinner together, when it was all ready. Once done, they went back into their tents to prepare and set out to find me. Zenix had her weaponry about her, consisting of a small sword and plenty of wit about her.

'Cindy, you stay here, and Renelle and I will go look for your husband,' she ordered.

In her best pitched whine, Cindy moaned, 'But I want to go with you. I could be of further use to you, too.'

'We are not here to 'use' people, as you put it,' Renelle said. 'We all work together for our common good. It's been like that for centuries!'

'Well said, Renelle.' Zenix thought heavily on the matter, thinking maybe it would be better to take Cindy along, just in case. After all, a husband and wife reunion was something to be relished the moment it happened. 'Okay, Cindy, come with us, and we'll go find Elias together.'

'Yay,' Cindy leapt for joy, thinking about her current status as my wife. She heartily joined the search party.

Some of the others in the encampment came over to take over Cindy's obligations and ate what was left over. They waved the party along, wishing them luck.

Zenix, Renelle and Cindy were still searching for me for over an hour, when a full moon lit up overhead.

The foliage was rich, and teeming with so much life, it had a life of its own. Hoots and hollered calls belted from the trees; the branches knew nothing else. Birds flew their many coloured wings in the enriching air that surrounded the forest. There were many hiding places too, which the animals took full use of. I guess it is why common folk like us and primitives had a rivalry, and everything was felt around a person.

There were times we worked together, but there were times we went to 'war'. *These were the latter times.* Zenix was guided by her hunch and wit; an advanced scouting bird or two didn't hurt matters, either. Their squawking helped her push the boundary between a young girl's loneliness and her fellow's potential demise.

She asked Cindy, 'You really love him don't you?'

Cindy swooned, 'He's wonderful. And he's a good and fair man. Unlike others I've come across in my time.'

'What makes him better than others?'

'I feel he's able to entwine logic and passion together in a harmonious fashion. He's a pilot now, but he's got this scientific kick about him.'

'So he's very enamoured with you,' Zenix surmised.

'I think so.' Cindy looked up at the emerging stars. 'He's much in demand in our world. We were in a simulator, which had gone wrong. I believe we'd gotten lost, then we woke up here.'

Zenix crinkled her nose. 'A simulator, you say?'

'Yes,' Cindy explained, 'We were preparing for space flight, you know, exploring and the like. Then we came across a storm, or some malfunction, and we ended up in your realm.'

Zenix nodded, as she, Cindy and Renelle came to a clearing. There were noises coming from the left side. Dwellings dotted the foliage with wooden likenesses of earlier designs. *Guess that is where our wood came from*, Zenix thought.

They scanned the envelopment and soon came across my happy, dangling self. Well, I was not going to be a damsel in distress, or even a soon-to-be scientist in distress!

One glimpse of me was all it took for Cindy, as she ran to me. 'Elias!'

She took a few steps in haste and partly in ambition. Zenix sensed a trap and prevented her from going any further. Renelle was prepared, and drew a weapon. They were surrounded by the Lesoos, who came out in droves; their Leader stood proud.

She taunted the newcomers threateningly. 'Now, who's coming to feast with us?'

'Oh, Elias, I didn't know.' Cindy took a few steps back.

I tried to show comfort in my peculiar position. 'It's okay, baby. I see you've brought Zenix. There's hope, yet.'

Zenix saw that Cindy would need a bit of help, decided that Renelle was not enough.

She activated a wrist-device and called the rest of the Dagji for help.

The Leader still rode that proverbial high horse of hers. 'So you thought you'd get away from us. You won't escape us again.'

None of us responded to the continued aggression, when one of the Lesoos tied Zenix, Renelle and Cindy up and provoked the bugs below to come out and enjoy another type of feast.

'You won't get away from this,' the Leader continued. 'You don't even know the meaning of the word freedom.'

'We do too,' Cindy yelled at her viciously. 'And it does not involve you!'

Good on ya, girl. Yet how can you fight her when you're all tied up like me?

The insects came up quickly and they tried to fight them off, when a loud noise was heard in the distance. A large mechanised, cybernetic vehicle came out. Manned by the Dagji, it proved to me that they weren't as primitive as I thought. It was obvious that in my earlier discussions with Zenix, she wouldn't give her cards away. *I wouldn't either*, if I had that kind of optional weaponry.

'Just a bunch of junk found up at the camp I reckon,' Renelle said, as she cleverly masterminded her way out of bondage. 'I'll go up and help out.'

'You do that,' Zenix replied, as she freed her own bonds, and gave Cindy a hand with hers.

The Leader was mesmerised by the vehicle and got distracted. Cindy and Zenix helped me out of my predicament.

'Looks like the Lesoos have a battle on their hands,' I turned a corner and hid behind a tree for cover.

'Let's take care of these people once and for all,' Zenix agreed.

Those insects didn't get to enjoy us in the end, and scurried back to the Pit, where the old books lay. They carried on feasting on the old, mouldy, smelly pages the Lesoos *thought* were important to them. They were just copies of texts they had available already, but it was against their whims to destroy the originals fully. It figures they would let a lower life form do the dirty work for them.

'Hey, I've got an idea,' I offered.

Zenix and Cindy perked up to listen. Renelle had made it to the over-powering vehicle that was decimating the Lesoos's grounds.

'Let's take those bugs and put them in those houses of theirs. Now, there was something to chew on,' I stated excitedly.

'How about we drive these people into their Pit? They belong with the old musty books,' Zenix suggested.

'That works. You'd have to coordinate your idea with Renelle in that cyber car thing,' Cindy thought aloud.

Zenix smiled at her. 'It's a mutational. We get by from throwaway objects on this land. Then, they're put together, and we keep them for occasions such as this.'

'So, you're not the primitive sort after all,' I commented.

'No, we're not,' Zenix said, as she lunged forward to the oncoming battle.

The *Mutational*, as it was now referred to, hulked within its massive bits and pieces of mismatched machinery, hastily put together. It went, all guns in, toward the enemy and roared out an encampment fire no one has ever seen before. The Leader was easily overcome by the Mutational, and ran toward her dwelling, which got brutally stepped on by the oncoming goliath. I secured Cindy, making sure she was alright, and assisted the other Dagji in the fight against the Lesoos, or what was left of them. It got intense by the minute and it seemed that everything was going well, when someone came up to me and hit me very...

THUD!

And then the sleep released us. It wasn't a fallow sleep, but it gave way to much thought. Almost delusion, it was not harmful. At least it was something I planned to keep to myself, and I trusted that Cindy would as well.

Dreams like these are intense and I didn't think she was willing to share the scenes with other people. Especially, if they took a turn for the personal, which I really think it did for her. When we woke up sometime later within the simulator, we were met by Pemur, Busdon, Twiki and Theo. Another person was there too, but things looked too hazy for me to determine this.

'Temperature's stable. Heart-rate good. You might need to wheel them into sickbay,' a strange voice spoke.

'Gosh, I hope they're alright,' Twiki beaded away.

'The doctor knows best, Twiki,' Theo encouraged, 'Let's leave him to work.'

Twiki left the simulator bay with Theo, as Pemur and Busdon got into the craft and tried to get us out.

I began open my eyes. 'Where, what?'

The disorienting delusions were fading. The pretty island-like environment was not there; I no longer saw Mutationals, Zenix, her aid Renelle, nor any other Dagji, or even the Lesoos. Everything seemed to be in order, when we last saw ourselves manning the simulator.

Oh Christ, it'd been all a dream!

'The doctor will carry out tests on both of you. Your vitals are important to us and you should be okay,' Pemur said.

'Cindy,' I called out, looking at her.

She started to stir once she got a nutritional injection, and found it hard to balance herself steadily, even in speech.

'Elias? What? Weren't we fighting the evil tribe out to get us and... oh, we're not in those nasty woods anymore.'

It seemed disorientation got to her too.

Pemur knelt down to her. 'No, you're not in any nasty old woods, or flee-ing from projectiles of the past unknowns. You are here with us, in New Chicago, normal time. You've come off with a slight bump.'

She asked, 'Like a bump in the night?'

'Likewise,' Busdon clarified. 'But the forces in the simulator were greater than we thought. I had no idea you'd be hurling into a bad dream. You might be able to get out into space itself, if you and Elias are up for it.'

'Maybe later,' I groaned, rubbing my achy head.

'Yay,' Cindy cried yet again; this time her joy re-emerged and there was no question as to who she would like to travel in space with.

Me.

I cried with equal glee, and gave her a quick hug, before Dr Wildock wheeled us away into his examination room. There would be a full phys-ical given before we, or anyone else, drifted into the great realm of space.

CHAPTER XI

It had been a gruelling few months more of training before I was allowed re-entry into the simulator for one last dance in the rocket. This time, only Cindy was with me. No assistance from Twiki or Theo was required. They were a great help, but were more crucial to the constant rebuilding of our 25th century society, helping to program future sentients.

Cindy and I remained together as one unit. It had been awhile since our initial meeting and subsequent marriage, oh, I gathered a year or so. We remained intimate and enjoyed ourselves immensely, mostly beyond the optical reaches of the prying eyes of the Directorate. Not that it mattered to them; I firmly believed it did not. My school days were over, and now I was to fulfil my dreams of piloting. Maybe to explore something no one ever imagined, like sitting outside a formal house with a piano by your side and singing. Our commitments to society went first, and at the moment, children were not a priority. Besides, I had to get Cindy to 'grow-up' more.

So, we slid into our space suits for the final steps in this long-winded dance and strapped ourselves in.

Pemur came up to the hatchway. 'Please Elias, no more blackouts, or sleeping binges. This is as real as it goes before we put you two into space. Got it?'

'Yep,' I affirmed, 'And don't worry. We'll be ready for it.'

'Good luck,' he tapped the hatchway to close it up.

Cindy and I were alone, belted in, and buckled up. It felt like a straitjacket, as I wanted to love her, just a wee bit more before take off.

There was a pause in the moment, and I said to myself, *to hell with it*, unbelted and lunged toward my dear wife for a final off together. I did not care about the gravity; the gravitational forces which plagued you when you are going upward and get sick from, if not careful. None of that had any meaning. I just wanted Cindy. A bit of movement happened in my moment with her, and suddenly, a countdown was starting.

'I love ya, Cindy, and always will,' I harped out.

'I love you too, Elias, now belt up, it's starting.'

I just had time to seat myself in and belt up, as Cindy commanded me. The familiarly crazy ride had begun, again.

3-2-1, the timer went.

The lift had patterned itself within normal parameters. A fake whoosh made it more realistic, as Cindy and I embarked on one more training journey, before the real blast-off was to take place for us. Yet, I had a blast-off of my own to think about with her.

Cindy checked the stability, while I laid in another simulated course, with the supposition that we were finally 'out there'.

But we weren't.

We laid flat as a pancake inside the deck, as the 'vehicle' wibbled and wobbled through another pretend space flight. I just couldn't wait to get out there on my own.

'Landing fuel full, trajectory low,' I announced.

'Flight omega peter, leap-solo-mean 1 point, 2 nodules past the glascon,' Cindy continued.

A voice suddenly hit our airwaves. It was Pemur.

'Roger that,' he said, 'But don't make it so flowery; your jokes are killing me! You know what to do.'

'Right,' I confirmed.

We carried on in our final pretend mission, just to see us off into primitive space. It was primitive, not by Anarchian standards, but by emptiness. Stars and planets revolved around the bend, like people do when they get hyper and lose their way in life. They just drift; only stars and planets drift in an intentional pattern. People's intentional patterns could change at any time a decision was made. My decision was to remain awake, which I certainly did this time. There was no loose panels this time, and the Dagji were a far away breed that knew no grounds in the first place. Imaginations looked silly by these standards.

I looked at Cindy, who was making figure charts and tabulating them with a calculator. She looked so engrossed, I guessed she remained as strong as she was in Anarchia.

'You okay there, young lass?'

She looked up. 'Yeah, I'm fine. Just getting these figures down.'

'Need any help?'

'Nope,' she stated confidently. 'I've figured out a flight path and the way home.'

'We are home. Remember, it is just a simulation. Only a practice session, but the last, yes?'

'I am duly aware of that, Cadet,' she addressed me in formality.

Cadet. What will she think of next?

'Let me have a look at that,' I snapped.

'Sure.' She handed me her paper tablet.

I was amazed at her observations and admired her work. 'I didn't know you were into space flight so much.'

'You didn't ask. Anyway, you said it's a simulation. I just jotted ideas on a piece of paper and drew what I imagined. Something that looks the part, without being it.'

'So these are just play-figures?'

'Yeah. I'm no mathematician. I just looked at the charts on the screen and went from there. You can be inspired from monotony, you know.'

'Okay,' I said, reading her work.

I thumbed through what she gave me and there was an anomaly I didn't account for. 'What's this?'

She turned to me. 'What's what?' Then she examined her findings. 'Oh, that's a hole or gate or something. Could link up to another quadrant or something. I just made it up. Doesn't it look pretty, with all the squiggles?'

I was astounded at her findings. 'You may have discovered what we've been searching for, for a long time since the Blast.'

I paused, taking it all in, then continued, 'Even in simulation, this may hold water. We need to see this for ourselves.'

'Okay.'

I gave her a kiss.

'What was that for? Discovering a silly-girl wife?'

'No, for being an unknown genius, Mrs Huer.'

A complimentary pause broke out, as the simulation wore on. It felt like we've been in here an hour or so. I was feeling it too; the pressure, the cramped space, Cindy.

'Okay, smarty-toots,' she riled on, 'So you think I'm a genius. What will that get us?'

The lady may have inadvertently discovered a path to another, distant galaxy that Mankind had never dreamed of.

Anything was possible. Okay, we may be visiting other planets close by, like Silage has done on Dracos, but beyond that, wow. *And she was so blase´ about it!*

'We can travel the stars like no other,' I said to her, 'Explore with mighty ships. Even on the way there, we could pass by Saturn's moon Dracos to see my brother.'

I got all excited about the possibilities this simulation offered us.

'I thought you disliked your brother,' Cindy replied.

'Well, I do,' I squirmed around a bit, 'But wouldn't it be a surprise for him if went to see him, as we were making history.'

'I think he'd shit himself if we landed on *his* planet.'

I was dismayed by her attitude. 'You really have a keen way with words, you know. Really dampening.'

'I don't like getting my hopes up,' she held the controls as if they were real. 'Besides, what will we find there once we are there?'

'Well, I don't know,' I argued. 'I figure we would go in and see him. Why, do you think he's on the prowl out there?'

'I am unsure, but from what I saw of Silas, he seemed like he was going up in their society.'

'Yeah,' I slurred, recalling our wedding reception.

We veered into another orbit and the simulator shook once again. A panel popped open and a small fire broke out.

'Damn, they don't make simulators like they used to,' I muttered, as I grabbed a nearby pod in the control section containing the extinguisher.

Cindy helped me put out the dying embers, and I sat down, frustrated. I was so sick of simulations and desperately wanted to go out into space. Gravity or not, I still wanted to fly! And fly I must, as I took the pretend bird for a landing. It wasn't the most bumpy ride down, but I was not im-pressed with the loud noise that accompanied such a windfall.

The hatch flew open and Pemur walked in.

'We've monitored your flight and everything above. Congratulations, Elias and Cindy. You are to become part of our Explorer squadrons.'

'Yay,' Cindy cried her usual baby-like utterance that made you blush at the top of the hill.

'Thank you,' I said, 'I trust we're in good order to disembark?'

'You may.' Pemur made room for us to leave. 'We overheard you during your flight. Please give me the notes you and Cindy were discussing. '

Oh yeah, those notes. I surrendered the paper tablet to him and gazed at her. She didn't show any displeasure at someone else examining her work, imagined as it was. It proved though that there was something out there to check out more heartily.

'I see you've mentioned a hole in this quadrant.' Pemur pointed at one of Cindy's drawn, scribbly notations.

'We think it could link us to other quadrants or galaxies. We think it's a gate of some kind,' Cindy answered optimistically. 'Reminds me of a past simulation we had here.'

'Yes, we try to make it realistic for you, so that is where your memory lies. I'll have this analysed at the lab and get back to you shortly. This may be what we were looking for,' Pemur announced happily.

'If that's the case,' I suggested, 'May Cindy and I go on the mission.'

'It'll be your first assignment in space. Real space.'

I looked at Cindy, who was going to do her cheer again, but stopped her before Pemur threw a gut at her.

'Nobody's perfect, you know,' she quietly stated.

'Well, if you found this supposed gate in space, then you my dear, are going to explore it,' he ordered.

Pemur walked away with our findings and we wanted something to eat. We made our way to the commissary. I was thinking about this simulation and what an accomplishment we might bring to the whole of the Earth, if there *was* a gate or hole in space. The past few hours were something else entirely, and I was entranced at what we may find out there, beyond our own star system.

He had the pad and its paper contents. Everything rode on them. I was also scared too, if it were a hoax and Cindy's imagination proved too fertile to grow any life with. I looked to Dad for encouragement and his wisdom for advice. I was really trying to be brave about the whole thing.

CHAPTER XII

In the weeks that followed, Cindy and I spent much time together before the big time into the stars, exploring. We walked along Basil Street, nearby the sophisticated Dual Range Shopping Mall. There were lots of malls in our district of New Chicago, trying to emulate past architectural triumphs. Some bright spark decided to resurrect the various, burned out complexes that hulked the skyline and made pardonable use for them. The Mall was one of the many uses that was planned, aside from office space and leisure centres. I couldn't help but think Cindy and I were soon going into the distance to follow a star, a gate, or even get to the bottom of that Januard entity. Everybody still celebrates the phenomena as if it were Christmas. We would be altering time and humanity's aim within: to pass through the barrier to another world, maybe even another dimension.

'For all I know Elias, it could be just a simple passageway that all our fighters and transport ships will take. Like common routine runs, I guess,' Cindy postulated.

'For business, pleasure or exploration,' I added.

'Gee, thanks for giving me *perspective* on it,' she mumbled.

I giggled. We walked on. She had a point, though. What if this hole-whatsit in the universe was merely traversed by populations long ago. We, by just discovering its presence, made a big deal of it, because there was nothing to make a big deal of. Our world still required a lot of attention, sought or not; the cities glittered on, fused with the ships we currently used within *our* star system. Nothing more and nothing less. We carried on rebuilding and it was a marvel at what was come up with.

And then there was Silage. Brother Silage. Or Silas, with an elongated 's' which a snake would love to sound out within his diaphragm. Oh, to think I even now glance a thought or two in my brain about him. Just a quick wonder of what he's up to, or whether the universe was his own, strung up by all the history lessons he learned as a child. It would be interesting to see if we'd end up enslaved by primitive passions and the endless tracts of old. I got a glimpse of them through my time in Anarchia, Arachnia, and the accidental sleep I had involving a group called the Dagji.

History was a wonderful entity in its own right, helping you understand yourself within a category of enrichment. The enriching part was knowing when mistakes were made; when it was a good idea to stop the nonsense that you're doing and change the world from it on a new course. I never knew if Silage understood this, or did he take it all in, just like that, without thinking of consequences of action and whatnot.

I did hear from him from time to time. His messages were short, but firm: *Hello, Brother Elias, How's married life treating you? Did you explore the lab yet, or did too many rats get into the poison? I'm certain there are plenty of things Dad left behind for you. Ha-ha. I've been well, treating Dracos like it was an open book of awe. I cannot get enough of it. Be well, Silas*

Little did *he* know I was to embark on an important mission for Mankind. What dear Silage did not know is what lay beyond our star system. A small moon off Saturn's ring-around-the-roses complex did not dispel the concept of 'out there'. He never thought of that at all. All he cared about was correctly saying a spell's incantation, perhaps to conjure up a female. A female loon more like, as I cannot imagine anyone wanting to be with *him*.

Cindy derailed my train of thought, which went over the cliff and onto an embankment below.

'Elias, let's go for something to eat, yes?'

'What was that?' I paused, still shaking mentally. 'Oh, yes, that would be good.'

I exited the reverie post-haste, when we entered a restaurant which had a calm, quiet ambiance. Not a place for a family with children; the music would put them to sleep!

'I cannot believe we're going on that mission,' Cindy said to me excitedly.

'Yeah,' I agreed with her, 'We'll be in orbit soon.'

Rather soon. It was like a date. We've been on them before, as a couple with intention. Wedded bliss did not change the atmosphere of having a good time together like teenagers; Cindy was the perfect one, while still living chronologically in her twenties!

When we sat down and ate, Cindy commented, 'I guess Pemur figured out those drawings I made.'

'All in the name of science,' I stated confidently, 'He certainly did, and because of those silly squiggles you made, you and I are going on a trip of a lifetime.'

'I wonder what's out there?'

'Multitudes of primitives, fighting for their lives, I suppose,' I kidded around.

'Nah, you can't be a primitive and travel like this,' Cindy protested, 'How do you know they even left their little worlds?'

'Well,' I muttered.

'I mean they could be trapped there,' she went on, 'They must be very lonely, thinking they're the only species in the universe. They do not know their neighbours.'

'Would you?'

'Elias!'

I laughed, as the other diners shot quick glances at us before returning to their own business.

'I mean, Imaging you and I living out there. Another world, beyond New Chicago. We could be famous,' Cindy continued.

'Or dead,' I surmised.

'You put a groovy damper on things you do,' she pouted.

'Just being realistic,' I shot back.

'Pessimistic more like.'

Her pouting was ongoing.

'Hey, let's not fight on the eve of a great adventure,' I said. 'We'll have a look and judge what comes to us when we can. There's plenty of time to make up your mind about it.'

'Yeah, I guess so,' she replied softly, putting her napkin down.

Later we left and entered a local disco. It may be the 2460s but no one could swing as good as we did. The music was loud, electronic, sometimes acoustic, but never dull. A screen commemorated 500 year old anniversaries from Earth's past, whatever which could be mustered. Memories were fleeting, but some clever person put together a compilation showcasing what we lost. We longed to gain that same momentum. We danced and grooved to the music and a few bars of chocolate were sent out toward the young ones, along with the cool sound that went with it. We had a great time, and later when we got home at 1am, our evening didn't end there.

'Cindy, break out the champagne,' I suggested.

'Not enough excitement for you then?'

'With you, there's never enough excitement.'

The bottle was acquired and I popped the cork. It flew across the room, as I poured out the liquid refresher.

'To us,' I toasted.

'To a successful mission in space,' she answered.

We were inebriated with youth, as we drank some in these wee hours. It felt good, but then, I remembered. *Gosh, the mission.* It wouldn't be long before we were suited, booted, and strapped into a little telescope and *poof!* We were about to enter a different world.

CHAPTER XIII

The moment had arrived, as I snored gently in bed, during the early morning hours of July 3, 2464. *My birthday*; oh wow, a cool quarter of my life had gone in a distance. Cindy took hold of the silver thermal blanket tightly, snuggling into another one of her dreams. *Probably of me, of course, he-he*. She tossed the blanket off me, leaving me bare in the night. Or was it morning? Suddenly, the clock chimed on the half-hour, stating it was 4.30. *Ah, that'll explain it.* Cindy tip-toed her little fingers around my body, and the sensation was soothing, driving me wild. I got up, thinking I was dreaming. It was no dream. It was good ol' Cindihan in action. And for me, it was mighty fine.

We entwined ourselves together and kissed heartily. Really getting up to something, we were. I glanced at the clock again. 4.35. *Damn girl, why get me up so buckin' early? Buck this.* I dove into her like it was no tomorrow, as it wasn't tomorrow yet. It was just today. I fell apart at the seams, and let loose every passion I knew, or sort of knew naturally; I flung it all in her direction. It frustrated me that Silage would have been better at this by now, as passion was his greatest companion. With me, it was all science, logic, and the endless beading of Twiki that kept me going.

But now, I had a woman. *Did Silage have a woman?* I didn't know, but I cannot say otherwise, as I widdled and wibbled my way though Cindy, like when I first learned to talk. It was an exhilarating and scientifically sound experience. There were other times, but none like this one.

I decided to have more of that champagne from our early hours and got up to look for it. I checked the bottle and we finished it.

'There's another bottle of something if you wish,' Cindy stated.

'Okay,' I answered, and I went off looking.

I went to a cabinet and wondered what Dad had left behind. I searched the bottles, and one came to the fore. It was called a 'fuquwer', probably gotten long ago when we were just searching the stars in the early days, post-Blast. Cindy was all for it, and we got the glasses we used last night and had some of it.

'Here's to another year of life,' I toasted.

She figured it out, and ran up to kiss me. 'Oh, happy birthday, Elias!'

We washed out those glasses and poured out the subtle fuschia-coloured substance. *God, that was good.* It tasted lovely and subtle as a roving sunset protruding in on a romantic scene. Youthful inebriation had never been so certain, but it wasn't a high a proof as the champagne we had earlier. I guessed there would be a word or two on the subject, but I wasn't planning on writing the essay. That pace of wonderment I left to society, as I kept on digging and nibbling at Cindy.

With us refreshed out of our multicoloured, feverous dreams, it was about six. They felt great, and I was ready for the mission. It was hours away, but we didn't have much time to spare any longer. It saddened me greatly that it wasn't a weekend or an elongated holiday to embark upon. But we did have a honeymoon, and the yummy stuff would have to be put on hold, yet again. Still, we made do with the time we had and I prayed I made it count. I so wished the past ninety minutes would go on forever. It felt so rollicking, my mind floated on air. The ship we'd go on floated on something else. The fuquwer took its toll, but it didn't inebriate us too much as to not go on the mission.

A comm screen lit up. It was Pemur.

'Ready for the big day? We're all counting on you,' he said.

'Yes,' I shot back, frustrated our time was officially 'over'. 'Cindy and I will be ready in an hour or so.'

'Breakfast is on me,' he offered, 'Shall I meet with you at your apartment? I do not want to waste my finest pilot on himself or debauchery.'

We'd since left the family homestead in the Mackeon Fields area of New Chicago and lived in the spacious Dunne Flats complex in the Inner City. Close by the Directorate of any kind, I may add.

'Who me?' I gestured innocently to myself.

Pemur smiled. 'I'll come to meet you there.'

'Right. 0700. I know,' I acknowledged.

'See you then.'

I hastily switched the monitor off, when I noticed a countdown going inside my head. *Oh buck it*, I muttered past Cindy in the changing room and got dressed.

'Elias?'

'What Cindy?'

'Okay,' I answered, and I went off looking.

I went to a cabinet and wondered what Dad had left behind. I searched the bottles, and one came to the fore. It was called a 'fuquwer', probably gotten long ago when we were just searching the stars in the early days, post-Blast. Cindy was all for it, and we got the glasses we used last night and had some of it.

'Here's to another year of life,' I toasted.

She figured it out, and ran up to kiss me. 'Oh, happy birthday, Elias!'

We washed out those glasses and poured out the subtle fuschia-coloured substance. *God, that was good.* It tasted lovely and subtle as a roving sunset protruding in on a romantic scene. Youthful inebriation had never been so certain, but it wasn't a high a proof as the champagne we had earlier. I guessed there would be a word or two on the subject, but I wasn't planning on writing the essay. That pace of wonderment I left to society, as I kept on digging and nibbling at Cindy.

With us refreshed out of our multicoloured, feverous dreams, it was about six. They felt great, and I was ready for the mission. It was hours away, but we didn't have much time to spare any longer. It saddened me greatly that it wasn't a weekend or an elongated holiday to embark upon. But we did have a honeymoon, and the yummy stuff would have to be put on hold, yet again. Still, we made do with the time we had and I prayed I made it count. I so wished the past ninety minutes would go on forever. It felt so rollicking, my mind floated on air. The ship we'd go on floated on something else. The fuquwer took its toll, but it didn't inebriate us too much as to not go on the mission.

A comm screen lit up. It was Pemur.

'Ready for the big day? We're all counting on you,' he said.

'Yes,' I shot back, frustrated our time was officially 'over'. 'Cindy and I will be ready in an hour or so.'

'Breakfast is on me,' he offered, 'Shall I meet with you at your apartment? I do not want to waste my finest pilot on himself or debauchery.'

We'd since left the family homestead in the Mackeon Fields area of New Chicago and lived in the spacious Dunne Flats complex in the Inner City. Close by the Directorate of any kind, I may add.

'Who me?' I gestured innocently to myself.

Pemur smiled. 'I'll come to meet you there.'

'Right. 0700. I know,' I acknowledged.

'See you then.'

I hastily switched the monitor off, when I noticed a countdown going inside my head. *Oh buck it*, I muttered past Cindy in the changing room and got dressed.

'Elias?'

'What Cindy?'

She kissed me for luck.

I kissed her back in return.

We embraced and felt the early morning hours while away, as the sun began its streaky tone above the sky like a frying bacon strip. We bucked the early morning, and then we were done with it.

She was breathless.

I was dishevelled.

No one would look at us, potentially thrusting our forward rocket into space, toward the *whatever*; we did some of that here, on our own.

A quarter of an hour passed. Pemur was coming soon. *Yikes!* I ran and belted myself into the wash room to recall certain needs of *other* refreshment, when I put on a jumpsuit. Cindy had hers on before me.

Time knew no bounds and did not care to wait for anyone, even of consequence. Hourglass sand had a dreadful habit of slipping to the bottom. Reminded me of a song, when a knock came at the door.

It was Pemur.

I hastened my further dishevelment when I answered the door.

'Hi,' I gently waved.

'Morning,' he replied crisply. 'You know you leave in less than two hours?'

'I know,' I stated, fastening the nodules on my suit.

Cindy was ready to go. She had been for quite some time. Funny how things go differently in the 25th century; the women were usually the fast ones. Still, her time in Anarchia was a great help too, with the 'you never knew when' mentality.

She greeted Pemur. He acknowledged with a good morning. He kissed her hand. It reminded me of what Silage did at the wedding. At least I knew Pemur wasn't after her.

He asked her, 'Ready to do some exploratory research for the Directorate?'

She remarked, 'I think so. Looks a-bash, don't you think? Today is Elias's birthday.'

I blushed feverishly.

'Well, happy birthday, Elias.' Pemur turned back to her, 'The ship you'll be riding on is called *The Ancient Crab*, named for a pilot sent out long ago, who scouted our immediate shoreline.'

I chimed in. 'And now?'

'Now, it's your turn to go into the beyond,' Pemur said confidently. 'Make it count Elias, this could mean so much to humanity. The whole Directorate's watching you.'

We went out for a quick bite, as the time flew between us; many a birthday sentiment was toasted, this time, with tea and coffee.

Soon, we were in the loading bay, where *The Ancient Crab* lay in waiting. It was a Scout-class two seater pod ship with firepower, and good thrusters on each side. The cockpit resembled an ant's head, while the ship's fire-power was held in its side-bays. The ship did not look like a crab at all, but it wasn't big, nor small. It felt just right; any ship with a good thruster was fine by me.

I gasped at the sight of the ship, noting the reality of our situation. 'Nothing like the simulator at tall.'

'No, it's nothing like it,' Pemur instructed, 'It's a pure, fully functional, pre-programmed with the coordinates you need to reach, based on that drawing your wife drew up in the last simulation.'

My mind jogged a race. 'Didn't we fall asleep during that simulation?'

'That was the previous one. Oh, never mind,' he huffed. 'You're due to board in a few minutes.'

'Wow,' Cindy looked on, in awe of the massive ship.

'Some ship, eh? And you'll be in it with Elias,' Pemur smiled.

'Oooh, how romantic,' she cooed loudly.

'Now now, no funny stuff on that ship,' he demanded, 'You're here to work, not buck-in-space, although *that* would prove some interesting findings.'

She cried, 'Oh, can I find some for you?'

Sometimes Cindy could be a little too excitable for her own good. Pemur noticed this, but paid no heed. At least *she* was willing to go on this mission with me. No one else was scheduled for it.

'No,' he shut her down. 'Calm your nerves. I know this must be an exciting time of your life, but you'll have to endure the vastness of space and the atmosphere within the ship. You'll have to work to get there.'

Cindy turned to me, 'Huh?'

'Don't worry,' I interjected, holding her, 'It's just Pemur's way of wishing us luck.'

'Ah,' she accepted the brush-off, and boarded the *Crab*.

There were some people in the hall, waiting and watching us carefully, as Pemur spoke to them. They were mostly reporters and human members of the scientific community. The Computer Council Christmas light entities didn't give a phoo about what we were doing, but they did help program the ship. Even Clary Busdon paid us homage with hug and a good luck to both of us. Twiki and Theo were there too, but they were being used by the Directorate, and were not coming with us. It was a bone of contention, but Pemur had his reasons. I guessed he wanted Mankind to discover the *whatever* and give us full credit for the occasion. A minor detail was also awaiting us, which no one there wanted to give away.

I waved back at everyone present, as I entered the ship.

The enormity of it was just down to being originally piloting a simulator, and now we were piloting a *real* ship.

I looked at Cindy, who already strapped in, and made ready for take-off. I so wished it were her clothes.

I kissed her for the final time, before the feelings outstayed their welcome.

The countdown engaged, our hands were on the controls.

It chimed, *'3-2-1 GO!'*

The *Crab* boosted its rocket power, and suddenly, we were thrown into the dark void of starry space that was the universe.

CHAPTER XIV

Alone in space, we flew the *Crab* into an unknown wilderness. Not Anarchia, not Arachnia, nor even the Wild West of old. This was space. Space was a lonely background, but had a magic to it that couldn't beat Silage's yore for the genre. Still, he probably possessed some by now, and who knew what he'd do with such a discipline. The false night kept us company, albeit shy company. It was like being with a girl who didn't wish to give herself away too soon. Kind of like Cindy, when I first met her. The stars looked their best, as we whooshed through the familiar territory of our star system. We passed some orbiting moons from nearby planets, Dracos being one of them. I'd love to go visit Silage on *his* world to see what all the fuss was about and whether his dreams came to fruition.

We were already past Jupiter, and the last few planets of our solar system. The sun was far behind us, but a faint light told me it was still watching us in the distance. Uranus, Neptune and Pluto were sorry sights; their advantage, however, was to see into the vast expanse of universe. It almost felt like you could travel between New Chicago and New Manhattan, or even New London, and you'd still be in the same universe.

Suddenly, the lights blinked up on the on-board consoles; the pre-programmed coordinates became active. We were heading for the *whatever*. On the way, I noticed a strange shape in the distance, just floating around. It must have a trajectory somewhere; a flight path or something to get it going. I scanned the shape and it was a starship. It went pretty far into space, and soon, I saw the entity float back on a return journey to Earth.

I quickly scanned through my own memories, and realised it was the Januard, the entity we all celebrated annually when it appeared on our scopes, all around the world. This time, it travelled a bit too far out, but at least gravity pulled it back to its 'home'.

As I already had a mission to go on, I sadly left the Januard, and carried on with the task at hand. I was itching to find out what it truly was. *Maybe later.*

Cindy, who was also monitoring the consoles asked, 'How much farther are we? And what was that thing that passed us in the night?'

'Don't worry about it, I'll tell you later,' I replied, 'We shouldn't be much further from the *whatever*.'

'Looks like you discovered a different whatever,' she slyly commented.

'That's not the point of this mission, dear!'

She laughed, as I carried on probing the screens. A few button pushes later, a voice soon activated. *Well, I didn't do it!*

'You're 12 parsecs and 4 nodules off the starboard helm. The bow is fixed and you'll make it home for dinner,' a subtle-accented feminine voice rang out.

Cindy and I looked at one another in disbelief, and cried together, 'What the...?'

'I am the Megablastic Fantastic Computer,' it said, 'I was fed the stargate coordinates by the Computer Council into my database.'

'Ah, so it is a stargate we're looking for,' I noted.

'Yes, Elias Huer,' the all-knowing One stated firmly, 'We'll be there momentarily.'

'Wow, this ship talks like Theo,' Cindy sang in wonderment.

'Not like Theo,' I doubted the ol' girl, 'No one can beat Theo. Besides, it's a girl in here.'

Cindy fenced me. 'Doesn't mean computers don't know the difference!'

'Wanna bet?'

The computer took over the controls of the ship. *Complete control.* The ship barely made it intact through a small star cluster, not navigable to the human eye.

'I'm just as good as Dr Theopolis, even better. I can run this ship.'

A computer better than Theo?

'Ha-ha, very funny, young lady,' I playfully chastised the machine, 'Now what do we call you?'
A pause reflected a few seconds on the chronometer, when the voice answered, 'Call me Meg.'

'Okay, you know me. This is my wife Cindy.'

'Hi,' Cindy uttered, sitting back in her chair.

'Watch for the coordinates, guys,' Meg warned, 'You may be in for a bumpy ride.'

Soon, the *Crab* wibbled and bounced about, yet never losing control of itself. The rush of gravity was felt as small particles passed the hull.

'What are those?' Cindy pointed out toward the window.

'Small asteroids,' Meg answered, 'You may not be in its centre field, but there are some now and again that crop up in space. Take no notice of it, they're too small to hurt you. My defences are on full power. We'll be approaching the gate in 30 minutes.'

Good, then we'll see what this flying thing could do in the beyond,' I said.

There wasn't much work for Cindy to do, as previously predicted. Meg secured the coordinates and took all the data needed. She even went as far as communicating with the Directorate, though rudimentary. A quick message flashed on screen, then *poof,* it was gone. In her grasp laid the coordinates that will change all our lives, those in space and those on Earth.

'Ready, mark 3-6-9-12, Peter Alpha Lemur,' the robotic Meg called out.

I focused on my task; the aim to get through the gate. 'I'm ready for the handouts.'

Soon, I saw something that no one else ever imagined. Not in their wildly envisioned rides! A group of four stars guided us through a passage of light. They dimmed and danced, showing a horizontal light before they lit proudly, letting us through their passage.

They reminded me of orbs, but these were most unusual. A hazy, medium to dark yellow colouring surrounded us, with a small thunderclap-style noise to usher us inside. They flashed boldly, one at each compass-styled end. As we went through, I was thinking about the other ships that made passage through this star cluster. It must have been awhile ago, as this gate must have been here for eons! Maybe some human life passed through here, brave as they were. The alternative was that this journey would make the mark on Humanity, allowing passage to worlds we could never have imagined. When you are planet-bound, destroyed, and then planet-bound again, you would think to see what else was out there. Our solar system has some ideal places, but knowing us, we would want *more*.

'Amazing, isn't it? You're the first of your kind to enter this scope in recent times,' Meg congratulated me.

Cindy and I looked at one another.

'I think we've made history, dear Elias,' she said.

I felt over the moon, no. Over the world, or several, from this experience. There was nothing like making the history books, I'd say; getting full acknowledgement for something on this scale was priceless.

Meg wondered, 'Now that you've completed your mission, where to now?'

'I don't know,' I made a hasty guess. 'Let's have a quick look around, then turn back.'

'Okay,' Meg forwarded the controls, still playing pilot. 'Here we go, then.'

I felt redundant, as I looked at the light of barren particles in the new quadrant. It will take much of our resources to explore this region of space. *All in a day's work*, I figured. We piled on through the new quadrant like there was no tomorrow; it was as if it invited us in, yet we were still questioning its unknowns. What really made me proud was that I had my lively and lovely wife Cindy there to share our expectation. After all we've been through together, this was something to be cherished forever.

TO BE CONTINUED....

www.ingramcontent.com/pod-product-compliance
Lightning Source LLC
Chambersburg PA
CBHW050151110726
47898CB00008B/2755